I0703414

DREAM BITES COOKBOOK

DREAM BITES COOKBOOK
Cooking with the Commandos

SHORT STORIES BY *NEW YORK TIMES* BESTSELLING AUTHOR
KRISTEN ASHLEY

RECIPES FROM *USA TODAY* BESTSELLING AUTHOR
SUZANNE M. JOHNSON

Kristen's Note

Before we begin, here are a few things I'd like you to know about this cookbook.

The first is that the entirety of my portion of the royalties earned from this book will be divided equally among the Rock Chick Nation (RCN) charities.

RCN charities are, for the most part, women's and girls' charities that were nominated by my readers to receive donations accrued from a variety of activities I do with my Chicklets (Chicklets=KA readers).

That "for the most part" above means that we also give money to Bikers Against Child Abuse (BACA), a charity selected by me when I learned of the essential and tireless work BACA does for children who very much need a bunch of bikers at their backs. This selection was made after I wrote a book where my hero was a survivor of abuse from his father (Joker in Ride Steady of the Chaos series). That said, BACA was introduced to me by a reader.

The other charity, Black Girls Code, is a girls' charity selected not by my readers, but by my beloved nieces, one of whom is an engineer, the other a nurse. And both (and I wholeheartedly concur) feel strongly that all young girls should have the opportunity to be exposed to STEM (science, technology, engineering and mathematics).

You can learn more about the Rock Chick Nation, and these donations, called Rock Chick Rewards, on my website at: www.kristenashley.net/rock-chick-nation.

The other thing to know is that, if you're a new reader to me, or haven't been following me long, a hallmark of my writing is that I love my characters so much, I can't (and don't) say goodbye.

Therefore, there is quite a bit of crossover in all of my books.

I do this so I can visit with them.

I do this so my readers can too.

This book is no exception.

Therefore, for the initiated Chicklet, in this book you'll not only see the Dream Team, you'll get to spend time with some of the gang from the Rock Chick, Dream Men, and Chaos books.

I embarked on this project to give my readers a little something extra and at the same time make some dosh to do good deeds. So I tried to pack as much of a punch of goodness into it as I could.

Therefore, if you're a new Chicklet, see the end of the book for a reference of characters and where they appear. I offer this so you won't feel out of the loop, but also should you want to discover their stories.

Last, many writers write about things that are very personal to them.

I am no exception.

In doing that, I often imbue characters with traits or qualities of people I love.

Or I just base a character on someone I adore, full stop.

Over the years, as life takes its inevitable course, this practice has, on a number of occasions, become bittersweet.

Again, readers who have been reading me for a while know these stories, but many don't, and before you carry on reading the narrative of this book, some "inside" things need to be explained.

The first is that the character of Tod was based on a very dear friend of mine, Rick Chew.

Rick has since passed, eventually succumbing after years of battling cancer.

He was one of a kind, and if you haven't read the Rock Chick books, but you give them a shot, please know I changed not one thing about Rick. He was larger than life. He was loyal as fuck. He was funny as hell. We shared the same shoe size.

And I miss him horribly.

The second is that I gave my own cats to a hero and heroine in my Chaos novels.

At the time I didn't know that one of my babies, Axl, had cardiomyopathy.

I'm a pet person and an animal person. I've had pets all my life. And losing them is never, ever easy.

Axl, however, was that one fur baby you're graced to have in a lifetime. He was because he was not mine, I was his. He was my kitty alpha who claimed me and made no bones about who was whose and how much love he had to give to the one who was his.

And his loss broke me.

To that end, essentially in this book, I'm not only looking in the face of my beloved Rick, I'm also visiting Axl, who will live in the pages I've written, forever loved and happy in feline...and human form.

With that I bid you to enjoy what I wrote and the utter deliciousness Suzanne crafted for you. I had the pleasure of being a satisfied recipient in Suzanne's test kitchen for many of these recipes, and I tried out many of the others in my own kitchen and devoured them with glee.

In other words, I can assure you, you are in for a treat.

So enjoy.

And as ever...

Table of Contents

PROLOGUE

Coming Home

KA

fly into Denver International Airport, pick up my rental car, and fret that, after I leave Peña Boulevard, I won't be able to find my way downtown.

That emotion is wasted.

Time has flown. It's been nearly two decades since I left Denver. And when I did, I knew the Mile High City like the back of my hand.

But as my car cruises the distance, I find that hasn't changed.

I've made a life in other places.

But being in Denver always feels like coming home.

Arriving downtown, I check into Hotel Teatro, itching to head right back out.

Once I dump my bags in my room, this is what I do.

Get to Speer Boulevard.

Turn onto Broadway.

Go south.

When I near it, I search for a parking spot (not easy).

I then hoof it to that special corner on Broadway where it all began.

All of it.

The realization of my dream.

I open the door and the bell above it rings.

Immediately, I see there's a huge movie poster of *Da 5 Bloods* tacked over the shelves behind the espresso counter, this partly obscuring an epic collage of pictures of cats.

I walk to the line extending from the counter, eyeing the two people who are busy behind it.

I wait in line and finally make the front.

Of course, the gorgeous, curvy redhead who waits on me doesn't recognize me.

I pretend I don't know her intimately and order a Textual, the bespoke coffee drink named after the famous barista who is working next to her. His hair is wild, his beard wilder, and his manner even wilder.

He's now banging on the large, red espresso machine, creating his concoctions from what appears to be brute force.

He's doing this multitasking.

The other task he's performing is having an argument with a man with a long gray ponytail peeking out from under the back of a bandana wrapped around his cranium. A man who is all the way across the bookstore standing behind a counter.

"It's about where that damned red cap landed in the end, motherfucker," the barista is saying. "That's Spike's statement."

"I'm not disagreeing with you," Bandana Man replies.

Famous Barista returns, "Then what were you saying?"

Which brings an exasperated, "Man, *the same thing as you.* Spike Lee doesn't give you anything for free, brother. With Spike, you gotta earn it. And to do that, you gotta *pay attention.*"

Since I've seen the film (and the huge-ass poster is a big honking clue), I know they're talking about *Da 5 Bloods.*

The redhead gets close to the barista in order to give him a cup with a drink order, a heart with an arrow through it and several stars drawn on it with a hot pink sharpie (my cup has a stick figure alien on it made up of an oval with eyes, nose and smiling mouth, antennae looping from the top, with mitten hands sticking out each side and globs for feet).

"It bums me out when Duke agrees with me," the barista grumbles to the redhead.

That's when she looks at me.

And winks.

Indy Nightingale.

Winking at me.

My heart flips in my chest as I smile back.

Through all of this, I'm waiting at the end of the espresso counter to get my drink.

And when Tex, the barista, puts it there, I mutter, "Thanks."

He doesn't even look at me.

He starts banging on the big red machine again.

I grin to myself, find a seat in the seating area at the front of the store that has tables, chairs, armchairs and a couch in front of the window, all a general mishmash that is totally disordered and even more totally welcoming.

As I sit, I take it all in—the hustle and bustle of Fortnum's Used Books—and I do this while I wait for the large-ish round table in the corner to clear out so I can nab it.

This takes twenty minutes.

I don't even wait for the staff to clean it off.

I nab it.

I sit with my back to the wall.

Which is the perfect positioning for what happens fifteen minutes later.

The door opens.

The bell above it clangs.

Conditioned to do this after the many escapades that have happened in that store, and the books that are based around it, not to mention the quality of person that tends to walk through, everyone in the store looks right to the door.

Because you never know what's going to walk into Fortnum's.

And what might happen after they do.

All of us are immediately rewarded for our effort.

Because in walk four of Hawk Delgado's commandos.

Daniel "Mag" Magnusson.

Boone Sadler.

Axl Pantera.

And Augustus "Auggie" Hero.

They're here to see me.

CHAPTER ONE

Certified

Mag

One month earlier…

Mag was in the kitchen with a pastry brush in his hand when he heard the back door open.

His timing couldn't have been better.

Evie was home from class.

"Oh. My. *God!*" he heard her shout from the utility room.

He grinned to himself as he continued to brush garlic butter.

But he didn't miss it as she walked into the kitchen, book bag over her shoulder, eyes not on him, but on what he was doing at the island in the kitchen of their new house.

The house wasn't new, as in a new build.

It was an old bungalow in Wash Park that had a utility/mud room, a great kitchen, a dining nook, a groovy living room with big windows, a decent master, guest room, and Mag's favorite part, a finished basement.

They hadn't been there long.

And he was already drowning in Boho.

He didn't give a fuck.

It made Evie happy to OD on Anthropologie, Urban Outfitters, and vintage shops.

It also gave him something to give her shit about.

And he wouldn't tell her this (or at least he wouldn't until the time was right), but he actually liked it.

Outside the finished basement, which she'd declared his "domain" (and she'd used the word "domain," such a cute fucking dork), the kitchen was the best room in the house.

Wild patterned tile as a backsplash. Taupe-gray cabinets. Wood countertops and open shelves.

And lots of freaking plants (nearly all of them given to them by Ryn).

He'd balked when Evie had told him she wanted to buy a mint green SMEG fridge to pick up the mint green color the base of the island was painted.

In the end, though, he'd given in.

He'd made a habit of doing that when it came to Evie.

He didn't give a fuck about that either.

"What are you making?" she asked, eyes big and focused on the tray on the island.

"Cheesy Bacon Knots," he answered.

"Did I do something amazing I'm not aware of to earn this fantasticness?" she asked.

Fantasticness.

His woman was not only a dork, she was a nerd and a goof.

Certified for all.

And perfect for him.

"That blowjob this morning pretty much rocked," he told her.

He saw her lips turn up as she dumped her book bag on a stool by the entryway to the utility before she wandered to the island, her gaze now resting on him, doing all of this saying, "If it was that, I'd weigh thirty pounds more than I do."

She wasn't wrong about that.

She dug sucking him off.

And he seriously dug that she did and how she did it.

That said, he didn't cook his gratitude for her.

Strike that.

He did.

He made her breakfast every morning.

Something he did that morning after the phenomenal blowjob she gave him.

But it was usually Evie who made their dinner.

"Hawk's got a thing," he shared.

She put her hands on the island, her eyes still aimed at him.

Damn, she was pretty.

He'd never get used to it, how pretty his girl was.

He dug that too.

"A thing?" she asked.

"We do charity shit. It's part of our responsibilities. We have a certain number of hours we need to do a year as a team. We get together and pick what we do, commit to it, then do it. Usually, it's runs to fundraise. Five Ks. Marathons. We adopted a highway once. That sucked, but it was important work to do. Someone got wind of this, approached Hawk, they had a sit-down, and now me and Boone, Axl, and Aug are doing a charity cookbook."

Now she wasn't just looking at him.

She was blinking at him.

Rapidly.

"Sorry?" she asked.

"Some chick named Kristen Ashley, who's a writer, but she also raises money for women's charities, approached Hawk about doing a fundraising thing. Hawk told her the guys cook. She came up with the idea. Now Hawk wants us to give her recipes so she can compile them with a chef friend of hers named Suzanne Johnson, who's going to test-kitchen them. If the recipes work, they'll pull it together, sell the books, and raise money for some women's charities."

"That's the most preposterous thing I've ever heard," Evie blurted.

Mag started laughing.

"Why is the name 'Kristen Ashley' familiar?" she asked when he quit laughing.

"That's what I thought," he muttered, though it wasn't an answer because he couldn't put his finger on it, but every time he thought about it, before he could do something to figure it out, something else came up.

"I mean, how would she know that Hawk expected this of you guys?" Evie pressed.

Another good question he had no answer to.

Then again, his boss was far from an open book. Who knew who the man knew?

"No clue," he answered.

"Did you look her up?"

He shrugged. "Haven't had the time."

She headed to her book bag, probably to grab her tablet or phone in order to research the name.

That was Evie.

She didn't wonder about shit for long.

If she had a question, out came a laptop or her phone and she was tapping shit in to find the answer.

It came with having a mind like hers.

She was a genius, that was also certified (and not a joke), and in the time they'd had together, he'd found she just couldn't know *enough*.

About anything.

He dug that about her too.

Big time.

"Doesn't matter, babe," he told her. "We're under orders."

That stopped her progress and she turned to him.

"Under orders?"

Mag nodded.

"You, and your commando brothers, are under orders to create recipes?" she went on.

He grinned at her and tossed a hand out to the tray in front of him that was covered in baked pizza dough twisted up with parmesan and bacon that he'd just finished brushing garlic butter over.

"Are you complaining?" he asked.

"Heck no," she answered, moving back to the island. "Do *I* get to test-kitchen all your recipes?"

"Absolutely."

She glanced at the knots. "Then I don't care who Kristen Ashley is. I'm all for this."

Mag was grinning again.

And through doing it, he said, "I wanna add your Cinnamon Clusters to my list of recipes."

"If it's for charity, go for it," she offered. "What else are you going to do?"

"Mom's chocolate chip cookies, my grilled pizza, and these to start."

Her head jerked, her hair flowing with it.

Yeah, his girl was all kinds of pretty.

"Whoa," she said. "You're pulling out the big guns."

"It's for charity."

She was staring at him again, unblinking this time.

And she did it so long, he had no choice but to ask, "What?"

"I really love you, Daniel Magnusson."

When he heard that, no hesitation, he made a move, doing this toward her.

But her hand flew up his way and she ordered, "Don't!"

Was she crazy?

Looking at him like that and telling him she loved him, she knew that bought his mouth.

At least.

"Don't?" he asked, stopping his advance.

She tipped her head to the knots. "Are those fresh out of the oven?"

"Yeah."

"And do you intend to kiss me right now?"

"Yeah."

Now she planted her hands on her hips.

"Danny, I know you. I see the look on your face. If you kiss me with that look on your face, we're totally having sex on the kitchen floor."

She was totally right.

"And this is a problem?"

She repeated the move of tipping her head to the knots. "Those won't be warm after sex."

"I'll make another batch."

He could see her shift immediately to considering that.

She wanted to have sex with him on the kitchen floor.

Fuck, he loved this woman.

That meant he finished his move, rounding the corner of the island and pulling her to him with his hand wrapped around the back of her neck.

"One knot," he murmured, eyes on her mouth, "then we're having kitchen-floor sex."

"Deal," she murmured back.

Oh yeah, she wanted to fuck on the floor.

He reached out and snatched a knot for her.

Then one for him.

She munched, approving with her eyes.

He munched, thinking he didn't do half bad.

Then they had kitchen-floor sex.

KA

Fast forward one month…

I'm sitting at the table in Fortnum's with the guys.

And we're going through Mag's recipes.

We don't get through the first one (Cheesy Bacon Knots) before Auggie says, "Didn't you have sex with Evie in the middle of making those?"

I do a head jerk at the blaze of fire Daniel "Mag" Magnusson aims at Augustus "Auggie" Hero after he says that.

Man, I'm sure glad that look isn't aimed at me.

Yikes.

"No, it was after, not in the middle," Axl Pantera puts in smoothly.

Boone Sadler lounges back in his chair, muttering, "So this is how this is gonna go."

"One hundred percent," Auggie states.

"Fuck," Mag says under his breath.

"Gotta give the…what do you call them again?" Auggie asks me.

"Chicklets," I answer.

"You call your readers Chicklets?" Boone queries.

"Uh, it's an inside thing," I tell him.

He clearly wants to know no more because he doesn't pursue it.

Auggie picks up his thread. "Gotta give the Chicklets their money's worth."

"So you guys locker-room talk," I say, and I gotta admit, I'm kinda disappointed.

"Hell no." (Axl)

"Fuck no." (Mag)

"Absolutely not." (Boone)

"Not on your life." (Auggie)

This all comes at me at once, and it's confusing, considering what I just heard.

"So…" I say leadingly.

"I know because Pepper told me," Aug states.

"And I know because Ryn tells me," Boone adds.

"Same," Axl grunts.

Mag just nods his head.

This means Evie spills to her girls.

I start laughing.

"It's kinda not funny," Mag points out.

"It's totally funny," I disagree. Then add, "So you don't locker-room talk. But the women do, and you save it up to give each other shit when the time is right."

"That's about it," Mag says.

"*What?*"

We all jump when this is boomed at us from the vicinity of the espresso machine.

Tex is glaring at us.

Or, more aptly, glaring at the commandos.

He's also clearly not feeling like making them guess as to why he boomed our way because he continues.

"All you badasses waltz in here and sit down to have a chat, five a' you, takin' up space, and only one of you bought a coffee? What do you think this is? A community center?"

He takes a breath, but not a long enough breath for anyone to get a word in before he keeps going.

"No, I'll answer that. It's not. Get your butts up here and pay for the privilege of taking the corner table. Outside of the couch, that table is our top spot. Fuckin' A."

With that, he stomps the four paces back to the espresso machine.

As he's stomping, I'm pretty sure I see *Da 5 Bloods* poster ripple.

And I watch him do this, thinking happily that life can throw some serious shit at you, but in the midst of that, one thing you can rely on is that some things never change.

And that's a very good thing.

"Guess we have our orders," Axl says as he pushes his chair back to get up.

The others follow suit.

"You want another?" Boone offers before he heads to the espresso counter.

"That's sweet, but I'll save the table and get a refill when you guys get back," I tell him.

He waits half a beat.

And then, with a different look on his face…

One that I can only describe as a *commando look*…

No, not only.

It could also be described as a *Dom look*….

Niiiiice.

He repeats, "Do you want another?"

Well then.

"Uh, sure. A Textual," I say.

He nods and moves to join the others in line.

I study them as they wait.

Boone is tall, lean, blond, green-eyed, and gorgeous. Classic male beauty. Top to toe.

Mag is even taller, his brows are heavy, his dark hair is messy, his eyes are electric blue. He's kinda the boy next door with a hotness quotient of 7,550.

Axl has silver hair and striking ice-blue eyes. His features are rugged and there's an exoticness to him that even surpasses Auggie.

This is saying something because Auggie is all classic Greek good looks. Thick, arched brows. Black hair. Intense eyes. Hooded brow. Strong nose. And utterly perfect lips.

Looking at them, only I could think what I am thinking.

I did good with these boys.

I really did.

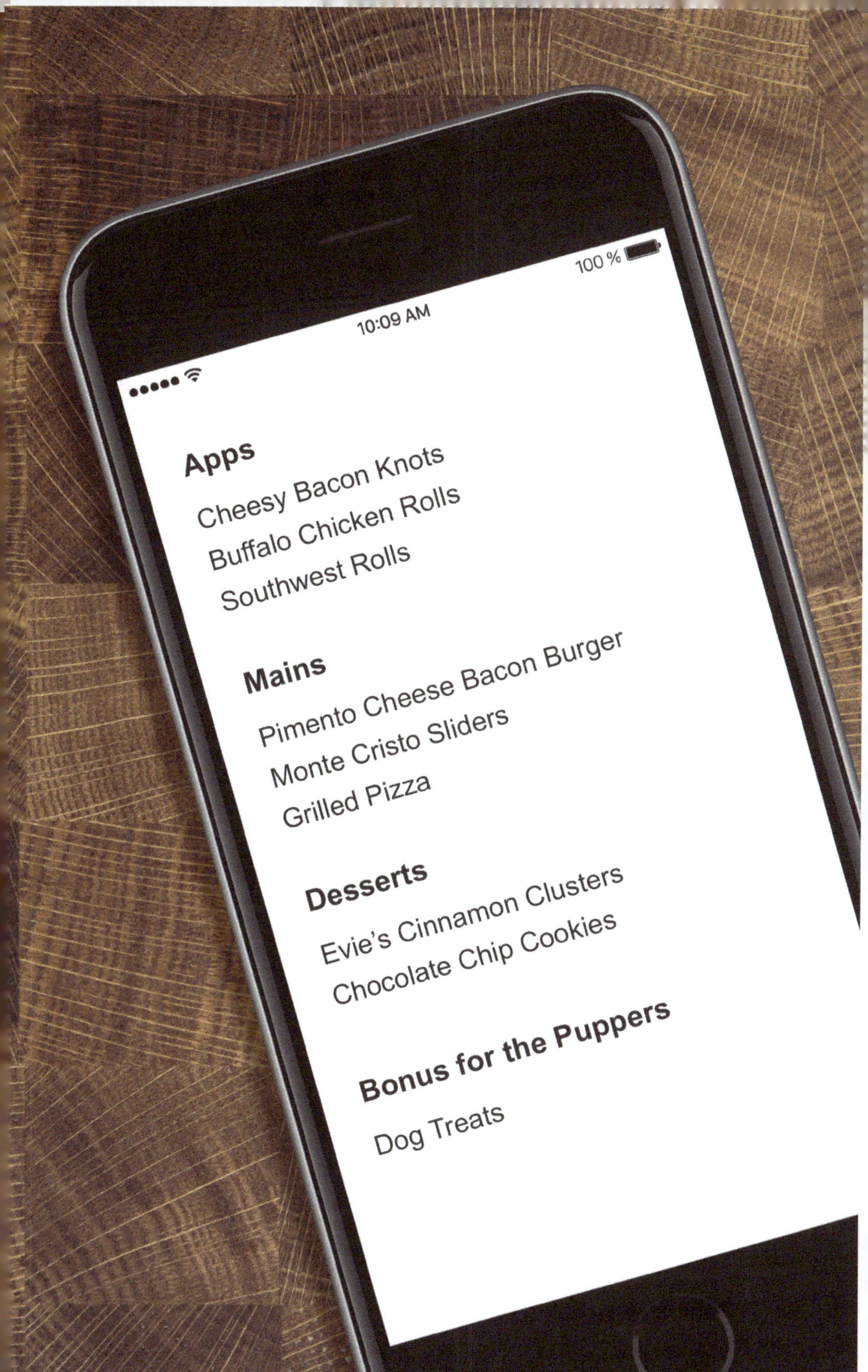
100 %
10:09 AM

Apps
Cheesy Bacon Knots
Buffalo Chicken Rolls
Southwest Rolls

Mains
Pimento Cheese Bacon Burger
Monte Cristo Sliders
Grilled Pizza

Desserts
Evie's Cinnamon Clusters
Chocolate Chip Cookies

Bonus for the Puppers
Dog Treats

MAG'S APPETIZERS

Cheesy Bacon Knots

1 package pizza dough

½ cup grated Parmesan cheese

1 teaspoon basil

1 teaspoon oregano

12 strips bacon

4 tablespoons butter, melted

1 teaspoon minced garlic

1 tablespoon chopped parsley

1 cup Boone's Garden Marinara
  (page 45)

Preheat oven to 425 degrees. Roll out pizza dough and cut into 12 even 1-inch slices. Sprinkle with Parmesan, basil and oregano to cover. Place a strip of bacon over each dough strip. Tie together to make a knot. Place the knots on a wire rack over a cookie sheet. Bake for 18-20 minutes or until bread is golden brown and bacon is crispy. In a small bowl, mix together the butter, garlic and parsley. Brush the knots with garlic butter and serve with Garden Marinara.

KA Note: I had these in Suzanne's test kitchen. Obviously, from the ingredients, you can't go wrong. And leftovers are perfect for breakfast. Yum!

Buffalo Chicken Rolls

2 (8 ounce) packages cream cheese, softened

8 ounces blue cheese dressing

8 ounces buffalo wing sauce

3 cups chicken, cooked and shredded

1 cup shredded sharp cheddar cheese

1 package egg roll wrappers

Axl's Ranch Dressing (page 69)

In a large bowl, combine the first 3 ingredients with a hand mixer. Then, add the shredded chicken and cheddar cheese and stir until blended. In a deep fryer or Dutch oven, heat oil to 350 degrees. Take 1 egg roll wrapper and fill with about 2 tablespoons of chicken mixture. Roll up by folding both sides in, then rolling to close. Place a small amount of water on the end edge and seal. Repeat with remaining egg rolls. Place 2-3 at a time in the oil and fry for 1-2 minutes or until golden brown. Drain on paper towels. Serve with Ranch Dressing.

Southwest Rolls

2 chicken breasts, cooked and cubed

1 cup black beans, drained

1 cup canned corn

½ cup frozen spinach, thawed and drained

¼ cup green onions, chopped

1 teaspoon cumin

1 teaspoon chili powder

1 teaspoon cayenne pepper (optional)

1 teaspoon salt and pepper

1 cup shredded Colby/Monterey Jack cheese

10-12 egg roll wrappers

6-8 cups of oil for frying

Auggie's Avocado Dipping Sauce (page 106)

Mix together the first 10 ingredients in a large bowl. Place the egg roll wrappers on a dry cutting board. Next, place 2-3 tablespoons of the mixture onto one egg roll wrapper and roll like a burrito, folding in both sides. To seal the edge, simply brush it with a small amount of water and finish the roll. Place sealed side down on a parchment-lined cookie sheet and repeat with remaining wrappers. Heat oil to 350 degrees and fry the rolls three at a time for about 5 minutes or until golden brown. Drain on paper towels, slice in half and serve with Avocado Dipping Sauce.

Pimento Cheese Bacon Burger

1 pound ground beef

2 teaspoons Steak Seasoning

1 batch Auggie's Pimento Cheese (page 102)

4 hamburger buns

8 slices bacon, cooked and drained

Sliced tomatoes (optional)

Sliced onions (optional)

Lettuce leaves (optional)

In a large bowl, combine ground beef and Steak Seasoning. Form into 4 patties. Preheat grill to medium and cook burgers for 10-12 minutes, turning halfway through, or until 160 degrees for medium (170 degrees for well done). Right before removing the hamburgers from the grill, place 2 tablespoons of Pimento Cheese on each patty. Close grill for 1 minute, then remove all patties from grill. Place each patty on a bun and top with bacon. Add lettuce, tomato, and onion if desired.

KA Note: In the Rock Chick Lair, my only outdoor space is a balcony, so I don't have a grill. I fry my burgers in a skillet, and if I need to melt cheese, just top the skillet with a lid for a minute or so. Et voilà! Yummily melted cheese!

STEAK SEASONING

1 tablespoon salt

1 tablespoon pepper

1 tablespoon garlic powder

1 tablespoon onion powder

1 tablespoon paprika

Monte Cristo Sliders

1 (12 count) package sweet Hawaiian rolls

½ pound thinly sliced honey ham

½ pound thinly sliced roasted turkey

½ pound thinly sliced Swiss cheese

2 teaspoons Worcestershire sauce

3 tablespoons Dijon mustard

3 tablespoons mayonnaise

1 stick butter, melted

¼ cup powdered sugar

Black and Blue Jam

Preheat oven to 325 degrees. Line a 9x13-inch baking dish with parchment paper. Slice rolls horizontally together as one sheet. Place the bottom sheet of rolls into the baking dish. Layer with ham, turkey and cheese. In a small bowl, combine the Worcestershire sauce, Dijon mustard and mayo. Spread evenly on the top layer of rolls. Place sauce side down onto cheese and meat layer. Brush melted butter onto the tops of the rolls. Bake for 10 minutes uncovered and 10 minutes covered. Remove from oven and allow to cool for 10 minutes. Lift the rolls out of the dish and place on a cutting board. Using a large knife, cut the rolls into individual sliders. Dust with powdered sugar and serve with Black and Blue jam.

KA Note: During the COVID-19 quarantine, I made these up at the Rock Chick Shack. Monte Cristos are by far and away my favorite sandwich (the Reuben is a second runner-up). I don't hit the sweet side of this sandwich (I tend to slather mine in mustard only). So I didn't make the jam. That said, the Hawaiian rolls, the fantastic sauce and the addition of turkey take this over...the...freaking...top. They're insanely delicious. And leftovers were just as good.

BLACK AND BLUE JAM

2 cups blueberries

2 cups blackberries

5 cups sugar

½ cup apple cider vinegar

1 packet liquid pectin

6 (8 ounce) jelly jars with lids

Puree the first 2 ingredients in a food processor or blender and add into a medium saucepan with the sugar and vinegar. Bring to a boil over medium, heat stirring constantly. After the mixture has been boiling for 1 minute, add the pectin and continue to stir for 4 minutes. Ladle the mixture into the jelly jars, leaving ½-inch headspace. Apply lids and place in refrigerator until set, about 12 hours. Transfer to a pressure cooker to seal for a longer shelf life. If you are not using a pressure cooker to seal the jars, the jam must stay refrigerated. Refrigerated jams are good for 3 months and sealed jars have a shelf life of 18 months to two years.

Grilled Pizza

1 package active dry yeast

1 teaspoon sugar

1 cup warm water

2 ½ cups all-purpose flour

3 tablespoons oil

2 teaspoons salt

1 jar fig jam

12 ounces goat cheese, crumbled

Caramelized Onions

1 cup fresh arugula

Olive oil

Heat grill to 350 degrees using only the left burners. In a small bowl, dissolve the yeast and sugar in warm water. Let stand for 5 minutes. In a medium bowl, mix together the flour, oil, and salt and add the yeast mixture. Cover with a towel and allow to rest for 10-15 minutes. Place dough on a lightly floured surface and roll out to ½-inch thickness. Rub both sides of the dough lightly with olive oil. Place on a cookie sheet to transport to the grill. Pick up the dough and throw it on the direct heat (left side) of the grill. Grill for 1-2 minutes and flip using tongs. You will see nice grill marks. Start building your pizza quickly. Spread fig jam onto pizza dough. Top with goat cheese and Caramelized Onions. Move the pizza to indirect heat (right side) of the grill and close. Allow to grill for 2-3 more minutes. Remove from grill and top with arugula. Slice and serve.

CARAMELIZED ONIONS

1 sweet onion, thinly sliced

4 tablespoons butter

½ cup soy sauce

In a medium skillet over medium heat, melt butter and add in onions and soy sauce. Sauté, stirring occasionally, for 8-10 minutes or until onions are caramelized. The onions will be a golden brown.

Evie's Cinnamon Clusters

1 stick butter

1 (16 ounce) bag mini marshmallows

½ cup milk chocolate chips

½ cup butterscotch chips

1 (12 ounce) box Cinnamon Toast Crunch cereal

In a large saucepan over medium heat, melt butter and marshmallows until smooth. Remove from heat and quickly add in the milk chocolate, butterscotch and cereal. Stir thoroughly and quickly. Prepare a large sheet of parchment paper. Scoop out 2 tablespoon-sized clusters and place onto paper. Refrigerate for 30 minutes before serving.

Chocolate Chip Cookies

2 sticks butter, softened

1 cup sugar

1 cup light brown sugar

2 eggs

1 teaspoon vanilla extract

3 cups self-rising flour

2 cups semi-sweet chocolate chips

Preheat oven to 350 degrees. In a large bowl, using a hand mixer, cream together the butter, sugar, and brown sugar until smooth. Beat in the eggs and vanilla. Slowly add in the flour while mixing on low. Then add in the chocolate chips. Drop 2 tablespoon-sized balls onto an ungreased cookie sheet. Bake for 10-12 minutes or until edges are browned.

Please note: Mag's mom makes these with butter-flavored Crisco rather than butter, and so does Mag. Evie, however, makes them just like this!

Mag

One month before...

His back was to the floor and Evie was moving on top of him, his jeans were at his thighs, her jeans, panties and red Chucks had been kicked across the room.

Their hands were linked and pressed to his heart.

The engagement ring he gave her that she never took off—not ever, not showering, not doing the dishes, not *ever*—was digging into the webbing of his fingers.

"Trust you to take the bottom when we're on the floor," she breathed as she took it slow.

Too slow.

"Baby, go faster," Mag encouraged.

She didn't go faster.

She said, "Trust you to put bacon in the first recipe you make up for a cookbook."

"Evie, beautiful." He drove up his hips, and he got too fucking off on it when she gasped as he did. "*Go faster.*"

But again, she didn't go faster.

"Trust you to do a cookbook for charity *at all.*"

Shit.

He was going to have to flip them.

"Evie," he warned.

"Love you," she whispered, her eyes filled with the meaning in her words aimed right at his.

Yeah.

He was going to have to flip them.

He did that and her reddish-brown hair spread out all over the long, narrow colorful Navajo rug she had in front of the sink.

"Trust you to take over," she muttered.

He grinned down at her before he kissed her, took over, and went faster.

It took it out of him, she was sleek and wet and had her legs wrapped tight around his thighs, but he got her there before he let himself come.

He was working her neck with his mouth when she pulled her shit together and stated, "We need a dog."

Although he had no idea what brought her to that thought, Mag had long since given up trying to keep up with Evie's brain.

So he just lifted his head and agreed, "Yeah, we do."

"And a cat."

Before he could reply in the negative to that, she kept going.

"And a bird."

At this juncture, he needed to stop her, and he did this saying, "Babe."

"You're going to protest, then you're going to give me what I want, because you're Danny, and I'm yours, and that's how it goes. So let's just move past the protest part, eat Cheesy Bacon Knots, and research birds and no-kill shelters."

She was not wrong with any of that.

Shit.

"Let's start with the dog," he suggested.

"Okay," she agreed.

Easy as that.

But that, too, was Evie.

Oh yeah.

He loved this woman.

Evie was curled up in an armchair that had a big, chrome dome light arched over the top of it, gabbing on the phone.

"I know, right?" she said.

And then she cackled.

She was talking to Ryn.

About the cookbook.

Her brown eyes strayed to him.

And the look in them...

Fuck.

"Our guys," she said softly into the phone.

Mag held his woman's gaze for a very long moment.

Then, sitting on their armless leather couch among a shit ton of fucking toss pillows, he cast his gaze down to his laptop and continued researching recipe ideas.

KA

One month later...

"What's your favorite recipe?"

This I ask to Mag.

"The Monte Cristo Sliders," he answers.

"What's Evie's?" I ask.

"The Cheesy Bacon Knots."

"Do you have a dog?"

"Yup," he answers. "And a cat. And a fucking bird."

I smile at him.

And Mag smiles back at me.

Dog Treats

2 ½ cups flour

1 teaspoon baking soda

1 egg

1 cup crunchy peanut butter

1 cup water

2 tablespoons honey

Preheat oven to 350 degrees. In a large bowl, mix all ingredients until combined. Roll out on a floured surface to 1-inch thickness. Using cookie cutters, cut out the cookies and place on greased cookie sheet. Bake for 20 minutes.

CHAPTER TWO

Not a House, a Home

Boone

Three weeks earlier...

"So?" Ryn pressed.

He really didn't know why she was asking.

If she wanted to take it on, she knew he'd say yes.

But he looked around the house anyway.

It was a disaster.

Eyeing it, his first thought was that his Ryn wasn't one to back down from a challenge.

And on that thought, he really took in the space.

Some of the drywall was punched in like someone had lost their shit and taken it out on the sheetrock. The carpet was old, worn, stained, and had to go. When whoever was there last cleared out, they took the light fixtures, the cabinetry in the kitchen and baths, the sinks, plumbing apparatus, and even yanked some of the copper pipes out of the walls.

At least it didn't smell like cat piss, like the first house Ryn had flipped.

Though he saw rat droppings, which wasn't good.

But no matter what a mess it was, there was a certain vibe to the place that he liked.

Truth be told, he liked it a lot.

It was roomy.

Open.

Rambling.

Big back yard.

And set on an elevation that had an unobstructed view of the Front Range.

This was why, even in the state it was in, the price tag was substantial.

She'd still rock it when she flipped it.

He looked back to his woman.

"You should get it," he said.

"*We* should get it," she returned.

That was Ryn.

To her, they were an *us*.

In everything.

He had his job with Hawk, she still danced for Smithie.

But when it came down to the important shit of life, it was *we*.

It was *us*.

And in this, her gig at flipping houses, it wasn't only emotionally true, it was technically true as well.

He invested money, and when he had time, he worked with her on her projects (of which she'd flipped two so far, but she had grand schemes to do more, welcomed hard work, had a good eye for the bones of a project and a better one for décor, so they'd scored big on both—that said, Cisco had helped in a way with the first, Boone just decided not to think about that part).

When his buds had time, they worked with her too.

Mostly, though, she'd formed a loose alliance with the Chaos MC.

Even though it was "loose," no matter what, when she was on a job, one or more of those brothers was always working beside her.

They did it only for lunch, they didn't take a cut.

They said it was their "hobby."

This wasn't a surprise.

For decades, Chaos had made a "hobby" of making sure women landed on their feet.

Ryn's alliance with the MC had started as a necessity. Not due to the needs of the house she was working on, due to shit fucking with her life.

The shit fucking with her life had ended.

The alliance had not.

Case in point, Hound, one of the brothers of Chaos and the one Ryn was tightest with (something that didn't surprise Boone, Hound was a wild man, and Ryn had no fear) wandered in.

He looked to Ryn then looked to Boone.

Oh shit.

"It's solid," he gave his approval. Then went on, "I'll take it outside," and he immediately walked his ass outside.

Boone felt his eyes narrow as he shifted his attention back to his girl.

"What?" he asked.

"How much do you like it?" she asked back.

That wasn't the answer he was expecting to his question and not only because it was also a question.

He expected to hear about a concern with the foundation. Black mold. Faulty trusses. Hefty shit that killed a flip's budget.

"How much do you want me to like it?" he replied hesitantly.

She moved, her wavy blonde hair swaying along her back, but his attention focused more on her hips.

Ryn could move.

Wielding a hammer.

Commanding the stage at Smithie's.

Riding his cock.

She turned back to him and pressed, "Does this kitchen work for you?"

There wasn't much in the way of a kitchen left.

Still, Boone felt a tickle in the back of his throat with the way she asked this question.

The kitchen was in the center of a big room. There was a family room area open to it. There were floor-to-ceiling, one-and-a-half-story windows that came to a point beyond that.

And beyond *that* was the view to the Front Range.

In other words, it fucking rocked.

"Baby, talk to me," he urged.

"This isn't a house, Boone. It's a home."

He didn't move a muscle.

"Could you be happy here?" she asked quietly.

Not a house, a home.

In other words, not a house, *their* home.

"You want this for us?" he asked.

"Do *you* want this for us?" she returned.

"I don't give a fuck where we are, your place, my place, the moon. What I give a fuck about is if you think you'll be happy wherever we are."

His woman was gorgeous, flat-out beautiful.

But that look on her face right now?

Staggering.

Her response was, "I want you to have the kitchen you want because you love to cook."

His first thought was to order her to get her ass to him immediately.

But if she did, they'd be fucking on rat droppings and that shit wasn't going to happen.

"Are you sayin' with this that Hound knew you were gonna pitch this as our place before I knew that shit?" he asked instead.

She shot him a big, white smile, and he saw the tension ease out of her shoulders.

She wanted this for them.

She wanted to build a life with him there.

Raise their kids there.

Christ, he wished he'd brought the ring he'd gone out with Mag to buy a few weeks ago when he'd met her there that day.

He didn't care about rat droppings.

This would have been the perfect timing.

He'd have to find another.

Maybe when they first walked in after they closed.

"Right then," he said softly. "You gonna design me the perfect kitchen, baby?"

"Absolutely."

Of course she was.

Knock herself out doing it.

That was his Ryn.

"Right to the soul, love you, Ryn," he told her.

That got him another big, white smile, though this one was wobbly.

"Right back at cha, baby," she replied.

KA

Three weeks later…

"**N**o shit? You found your house in the middle of this cookbook business?" I ask.

Boone tipped up his chin. "Close on it next week."

"Only dude I know whose woman gets him a house based on the kitchen she's gonna make him cook in," Auggie, who I was noticing has the habit, instantly starts giving shit.

"Like you're not the cook of the family," Mag retorts.

But Auggie is Teflon.

And as such, not missing a beat, he shoots back, "Kitchen time is Juno-and-Me time."

"You didn't make up your pork rind nachos with Juno," Axl points out.

Say…

What?

"Wait, hold the phone," I cut in. "*Pork rind nachos?*"

I mean, it's a constant threat, imminent orgasm, just sitting and rapping with these dudes.

But…

Pork rind nachos?

That has to be the numero uno culinary orgasm *of all time.*

"They don't hold a candle to Axl's pulled pork tacos with peach salsa," Mag asserts.

Although that sounds *awesome*, nothing beats pork rinds.

I know that and I haven't even tasted them (yet).

I decide not to share that.

Instead, I say, "Please, I beg you, tell me those nachos are among the recipes you're giving to me."

Auggie's smile is wide and glamorous.

And his answer is perfection.

"Of course."

I hope a fraction of the sheer amount of gratitude I have for this is offered to him from my eyes before I turn to Boone and say, "Good call, avoiding any hanky-panky on top of rat droppings."

Boone sizes me up like he hasn't been sitting with me for the last half an hour.

When he finishes doing that, he says, "Christ, it's like you could be one of them."

"One of what?" I ask.

"Rock Chick or Dream Team, take your pick," he answers.

He has *no idea*.

"That's OG for the women who started it all, the Rock Chicks, and the next gen, which are our women, the Dream Team," Axl helpfully, but unnecessarily, explains.

"Unh-hunh," I reply.

"She doesn't get it," Auggie mutters.

There is no way humanly possible I could get it any more than I already got it.

I don't share that either.

"Magnusson!"

We hear this from the direction of the book counter.

We all look that way to see bandana-sporting Duke staring at the front door.

So we all look to the front door just in time for the bell over it to ring.

"Fuck," Mag mutters.

But my heart just...

Stops.

Because in comes two people I know very well.

Daisy Sloan (and she brings with her her mile-high, teased out, platinum-blonde hair and massive bazungas, their cleavage bared over a gingham print, cap-sleeved blouse knotted under her impressive rack, high-waisted, sailor-front, denim short-shorts, and cork-heeled-and-soled, brown leather, platform, six-inch strappy sandals).

And with her is Tod.

Half of Tod and Stevie.

Though now he's *sans* Stevie, with Daisy, and homed in on Mag.

Um…

Neither Daisy nor Tod waste time bearing down on our table.

More aptly in Tod's case, on Mag.

"Hey, sugars," Daisy greets, then her twinkling blue eyes (also curious in that "Do I know you?" way) hit mine.

None of us gets the chance to respond to Daisy.

Tod is addressing Mag.

"I see the memo has been lost," he states.

"Listen, dude—" Mag tries.

That's as far as he gets.

Tod jerks a thumb at himself and declares, "*I* am *the official* wedding planner to all Rock Chicks."

"Technically, our women are Dream Team," Axl notes.

Tod's attention shifts to Axl.

EEK!

"I'll amend, all Rock Chicks and *any and all* offshoots of Rock Chicks, of which the Dream Team *is*, seeing as Lottie is Jet's sister, Lottie is the Queen Bee of the Dream Team, and Jet *is a Rock Chick*," Tod explains like it pains him greatly to do so. "Be they here, in Denver, or elsewhere, say, LA. But definitely *here* in *Denver* where, incidentally, *I live*, and as such, know *all* the best venues and vendors to create *the perfect* individually-crafted nuptials *of all time*," he finishes.

He then slams down on the table something I haven't noticed he was carrying.

It's a scrapbook.

A massive one.

And it's bulging out the sides with wisps of fabric, color cards, what appear to be magazine clippings, and other bits of paper.

"This is what I've worked up so far," he states.

"So far," Auggie mutters with amusement.

Again, Tod's attention shifts. "Did I request comments from the peanut gallery?"

"Nope," Auggie replies, grinning broadly.

"It's good you're cute or you'd be on my last nerve. Since you're cute, you're on my *second* to last nerve," Tod shares to Auggie, and then looks back to Mag. "Your woman isn't returning my calls."

It's evident physically that Mag is at this point only very cautiously wading in.

He does it saying, "Well, bro, she reported in to me, so I know you had your preliminary sit-down, and you nixed her bohemian theme so I'm not sure where you two can go from here."

We all lean away a bit when Tod shrieks, "*I can do bohemian!*"

In the wake of that, everyone decides it best not to reply.

"Jet's wedding had a fucking *hayride*," Tod goes on. "And I *rocked that*."

"He totally did. It was fabulous," Daisy puts in with a pretty, sugary Southern drawl.

"It just has to be *chic* bohemian," Tod adds.

"I think that's the rub, man," Mag tells him. "She's all about the environment. It all has to be reusable and biodegradable and ethically sourced and sustainable and—"

Mag gets no further when Tod's eyes roll to the ceiling so that he can ask God, "Why do these women test me?"

"I can see you're worked up," Mag continues.

Tod's eyes roll back, and he inquires, "Oh? You can?"

Mag's lips twitch.

Tod's eyes get squinty.

Mag perseveres.

"But, just sayin', this scrapbook alone would make her head explode at the waste."

He then waves a long-fingered, very attractive hand at the scrapbook.

"Most of that are remnants *or* it's recyclable," Tod retorts. "If not used there, it'd be tossed. So at least it's being used. She can't have a problem with that."

"I'll put in a word," Mag offers.

"Put in two, or maybe seventeen, or however many are needed," Tod orders. "When planning a wedding *there is not a moment to waste*."

Mag clearly thinks his best bet is just to nod, which is what he does.

Tod looks to me, and my heart stops again.

He takes me in as best he can since most of the table is hiding me, and demands, "Who are you?"

"Um..." I don't quite start.

"I love your lipstick, sugar," Daisy says to me.

"Thanks. Chanel long-wearing," I tell her.

"Love Chanel," Daisy replies. "That red really suits you."

I grin at her.

"It's not just the lipstick. It's the overall look," Tod shares, and his appreciation is clear.

"Wow, thanks," I say. "I'll tell my stylist you approve."

"Your stylist?" Tod asks.

"Her name is Malia," I tell him.

"You do that. You tell Malia she's got talent," he says, then turns to Mag, pointing at me. "See? Look at her. She's all rock 'n' roll and edgy, but sophisticated. That...is...*chic*. And a talented stylist pulling that together? Stawp."

On that, apparently feeling his message has been conveyed, though I'm not certain it is, he turns and strolls out.

Incidentally, leaving the scrapbook behind.

"Since I'm his ride, guess that's my cue. Also guess I don't get any coffee. *Byeeee*," Daisy says.

And on a giggle that sounds like tinkling bells, she's gone too.

"I love this place," I declare after the door shuts on her short-shorted ass.

The only reply I get is from Boone.

And it's, "Jesus."

So of course, yet again, I start laughing.

It's that or start crying.

And in those stakes, I'll always pick the first.

Because when you lose something that means everything to you, memories of it are bittersweet.

But the bitter always fades.

And all you have left is sweet.

Even if it's shrieking about wedding planning.

"So you wanna go over what I cooked up?" Boone offers.

I focus on him.

And answer, "Absolutely."

APPETIZERS

Bruschetta with Caramelized Onions and Mushrooms
Jala' Poppin' Bites with Blueberry Pepper Jelly

SIDES

Cobb Wedge with Blue Cheese Dressing
Smoked Mac and Cheese

MAINS

Bacon Wrapped Steak Kabobs
Boone's Lasagna (the Chefy Kind)
Ryn's (Momma's) Lasagna (the Cheat and Eat Kind)
Ryn's Momma's Homemade Caesar Salad
Smoked Boston Butt
Filet with Blue Cheese Sauce

DESSERTS

Bacon Cinnamon Rolls

BOONE'S APPETIZERS

Bruschetta with Caramelized Onions and Mushrooms

1 French baguette

6 tablespoons butter, softened

1 cup sliced button mushrooms

1 cup thinly sliced sweet onion

1 cup soy sauce

½ cup freshly grated Parmesan cheese

½ cup Balsamic Glaze

Slice the baguette into 1-inch slices. Spread each slice with softened butter, reserving 4 tablespoons for sauté pan. Place baguette slices on a cookie sheet butter side up. Bake at 400 degrees for 2-3 minutes or until toasted. Remove from oven and place on a serving platter. In a medium skillet over medium heat, melt remaining butter and add mushrooms, onions, and soy sauce. Sauté, stirring occasionally, for 8-10 minutes or until onions are caramelized. The mushrooms will be a dark brown and the onions will be a golden brown. Remove from heat and place 1-2 tablespoons on each slice of baguette. Sprinkle Parmesan over each slice and drizzle 1 teaspoon of Balsamic Glaze to finish each bruschetta.

BALSAMIC GLAZE

2 cups balsamic vinegar

¼ cup brown sugar

In a small pot over low heat, stir together the balsamic vinegar and brown sugar. Bring to a boil and simmer for 15-20 minutes or until reduced by half.

Jala' Poppin' Bites with Blueberry Pepper Jelly

2 fresh jalapeños, diced

1 (8 ounce) block cream cheese

1 cup grated sharp cheddar cheese

2 tablespoons mayonnaise

1 teaspoon salt

1 teaspoon pepper

1 teaspoon garlic powder

2 cups dry hush puppy mix

2 eggs

½ cup milk

3 cups panko breadcrumbs

3 cups oil, for frying

1 jar Auggie's Blueberry Pepper Jelly (page 103)

Mix together the first 7 ingredients and form into 1-inch balls. Roll each ball in dry hush puppy mix and place on a cookie sheet. Place in the freezer for 30 minutes to harden. In a small bowl, whisk together the 2 eggs with the milk. Dredge each ball in the egg mixture and then roll in a pan of panko breadcrumbs. In a Dutch oven or deep fryer, bring the oil to 350 degrees and place 2-3 balls at a time into the oil. Fry for 1-2 minutes then place on paper towels to drain. Repeat with the remaining balls then serve with the Blueberry Pepper Jelly.

SJ Note: This recipe came to life one evening when I was making a favorite recipe of mine called Jala' Poppin' Chicken. It is the wonderfulness from above but stuffed to the fullest inside chicken breasts. Anyway, that evening I had too much filling and didn't want to waste it...it's that good. So I whipped up these beauties and never looked back. I love it when the test kitchen happens on a random night. SO MUCH FUN!

Cobb Wedge with Blue Cheese Dressing

1 cup sour cream

1 cup mayonnaise

1 teaspoon Worcestershire sauce

¼ cup milk

1 teaspoon salt

1 teaspoon pepper

1 teaspoon garlic powder

½ cup crumbled blue cheese

1 head romaine lettuce, cut into fourths

2 hard-boiled eggs, cut in half lengthwise

8 strips bacon, cooked and crumbled

12-15 Butter Croutons

In a small bowl, combine the first 8 ingredients and refrigerate for at least 1 hour before dressing the salad.

BUTTER CROUTONS

6 slices stale white sandwich bread, crusts removed, cut into ½-inch pieces

2 tablespoons butter, melted

1 teaspoon salt

Preheat oven to 350 degrees. In a large bowl, toss bread cubes in butter and salt. Arrange evenly on a cookie sheet and bake for 20 minutes, tossing at 10 minutes and 15 minutes to ensure even cooking.

To assemble salad:

Place ¼ head of romaine on a plate. Top with 1 egg half, crumbled bacon, Butter Croutons, and blue cheese dressing.

Smoked Mac and Cheese

1 box elbow macaroni

5 tablespoons butter, divided

2 tablespoons flour

1 cup heavy cream

1 cup milk

1 cup shredded sharp cheddar cheese

1 cup shredded smoked Gouda

1 (8 ounce) block cream cheese

24 butter crackers

½ cup grated Parmesan

2 teaspoons salt

1 teaspoon pepper

Preheat oven to 350 degrees. Bring 4 cups of salted water to a boil. Add pasta and continue to boil for 8-10 minutes or until the pasta is cooked through. Drain pasta and set aside. In a medium saucepan over low heat, melt 3 tablespoons butter and gradually whisk in the flour until a roux forms. Add the heavy cream and milk, whisking constantly until thickened. Then, stir in the cheddar cheese, smoked Gouda, and cream cheese. After you have a smooth cheese sauce, stir in the pasta. In a large resealable bag, add in the crackers and grated Parmesan. Crumble crackers using your hands or a rolling pin. Add the remaining 2 tablespoons melted butter and toss to coat. Pour pasta into a 9x13-inch baking dish and top with cracker crumbs. Bake for 20 minutes and serve.

KA note: I made this in the Rock Chick Lair. I ate this. I now fear making this again because this cheese sauce is so flavorful, rich and creamy, I might not bother with pasta, or anything else, and just spoon it up from the pan.

So, after texting my delight about this to Suzanne, we agreed there are many alternate uses of this cheese sauce. Including spreading it over veggies...and using it as a dip. When you try this, you'll want to keep the ingredients in stock for whatever you dream up to use the sauce for. It is just that sublime.

Bacon Wrapped Steak Kabobs

2 (4-6 ounce) filet mignon, cut into 1-inch cubes

1 teaspoon salt

1 teaspoon pepper

2 cups whole button mushrooms, stems removed

1 onion, sliced into 1-inch squares

½ cup soy sauce

½ cup honey

1 pound bacon, cut into 2- or 3-inch pieces

10-15 kebab sticks, soaked in water

Season steak with salt and pepper. In a large resealable bag, place the steak, mushrooms and onions, then top with the soy sauce and honey. Seal the bag and massage for 1 minute to ensure all of the ingredients are coated with the marinade. Refrigerate and marinate for 1 hour. Thread the skewers as follows: wrap a piece of bacon around one piece of steak, thread onto skewer, add one mushroom, then place one onion slice next. Repeat this order until the skewer is full. Place on a baking sheet until all the kebabs are complete. Preheat grill to 350 degrees and place the kebabs over indirect heat. Grill for 10-15 minutes, turning once. Place on direct heat and grill for 1-2 minutes, then remove from grill.

Boone's Lasagna (the Chefy Kind)

1 (32 ounce) container ricotta cheese

1 cup freshly grated Parmesan cheese

½ cup Basil Pesto

1 batch Garden Marinara

1 pound ground beef, cooked and drained

1 batch Homemade Pasta, cut into 3 9x13-inch sheets

2 cups freshly grated mozzarella cheese

In a large bowl, mix together the ricotta cheese, Parmesan cheese, and basil pesto. In a large saucepan, add the Garden Marinara and ground beef and simmer for 30 minutes. In a 9x13-inch baking dish, place 1 cup of meat sauce on the bottom to prevent sticking. Next, layer 1 sheet of pasta, 2-3 cups of meat sauce, 1 sheet of pasta, ricotta mixture, 1 sheet of pasta, remaining meat sauce and top with the mozzarella cheese. Bake for 50 minutes, remove from oven and let sit for 10 minutes before slicing.

BASIL PESTO

2 cups fresh basil leaves

2 tablespoons minced garlic

¼ cup pine nuts

½ cup freshly grated Parmesan

½ teaspoon salt

½ teaspoon pepper

⅔ cup olive oil

Add all ingredients except olive oil to a food processor. Pulse until coarsely chopped. Turn to low and slowly add in olive oil. Process until smooth.

GARDEN MARINARA

12 ripe Roma tomatoes

1 (28 ounce) can whole peeled
San Marzano tomatoes, undrained

¼ cup olive oil

1 onion, diced

2 celery ribs, diced

2 tablespoons minced garlic

1 tablespoon tomato paste

1 teaspoon salt

2 teaspoons sugar

1 teaspoon dried basil

1 teaspoon dried oregano

1 tablespoon dried parsley

1 teaspoon white wine vinegar

In a large pot with 4-6 cups of water, add in Roma tomatoes. Bring to a boil for 1 minute, then remove from heat. Pour off hot water and replace with cold water. Allow to cool. Remove the tops of the tomatoes with a knife and peel off all remaining skin. Add to a food processor with the can of undrained San Marzano tomatoes. Pulse on low until completely pureed. In a Dutch oven over low heat, add the olive oil, onion, celery and garlic. Simmer for 10-15 minutes or until translucent and tender. Stir in tomato paste until blended. Add in tomatoes and remaining ingredients. Simmer for 2 hours, stirring frequently.

HOMEMADE PASTA

6 cups all-purpose flour

6 whole eggs

Place the flour on a clean, flat surface and make a well in the middle. In a bowl, beat the eggs, then pour into the well of flour. Slowly incorporate the flour in the eggs to begin forming the dough. Continue to knead until the dough comes together and is smooth. Divide dough into 2 portions and wrap with plastic wrap. Allow to rest for 1 hour. Roll out dough on a floured surface until very thin. You should almost be able to see through it. If you have a pasta machine, follow the directions for your desired pasta. If you do not, simply use a pizza cutter and cut strips to the thickness you prefer. Allow to dry on a floured surface for about 5-10 minutes.

Ryn's (Momma's) Lasagna (the Cheat and Eat Kind)

1 pound ground beef

Salt

Pepper

1 (24 ounce) jar Ragu

1 teaspoon minced garlic (optional)

1 teaspoon dried oregano (optional)

½ teaspoon red pepper flakes (optional)

1 small container cottage cheese

2 (8 ounce) packages grated mozzarella (or grate your own or
use one package (2-4 cups depending on how cheesy you like things,
I like CHEESE!)

2 eggs (hard-boiled and chopped)

1 box lasagna noodles

Several pinches salt (for noodle water)

Put two pans of water on to boil, one big one for the lasagna noodles that includes a few healthy pinches of salt, one for the hard-boiled eggs. Hard boil your eggs, drain, rinse under cool water, de-shell when they're cool enough to handle and chop. As per instructions on the box, boil the lasagna noodles. When noodles are al dente, drain and rinse with very cold water. Handling them carefully so as not to break them, lay out on a clean dishtowel.

Preheat oven at 350 degrees and grab yourself a 9x13-inch casserole dish.

Brown ground beef in large skillet or medium saucepan having seasoned it with salt and pepper. Drain any excess grease. Add jar of Ragu. If faking it to make it and pretending to be chefy, add garlic, oregano and pepper flakes so your jar of Ragu might taste some modicum of homemade. Simmer this for a bit just so the flavors can coalesce, but not so long that it reduces.

Assemble your lasagna by starting with a layer of the meaty Ragu sauce at the bottom, then noodles (overlap the edges a hint as you lay them out), then spread some cottage cheese, sprinkle the chopped eggs, scatter some mozzarella, coat with meat sauce and repeat, until you run out of stuff, ending on meat sauce and a dusting of mozzarella.

Bake in oven for 25-30 minutes until bubbling and yummy-looking with the cheese browned. Let it sit for a bit before you dig in.

KA Note: Needless to say, the first recipe is Suzanne's, the second is mine.

You see, Suzanne created this lasagna recipe and I'm all for lasagna in any form. Bonus, I knew Ryn made lasagna in Dream Chaser. *Then I read the proof pages for* Dream Chaser *and was reminded that Ryn is no culinary dynamo, and she made the only recipe she knew, one her mother taught her. I also saw that I gave her the lasagna my mother gave me, except I bastardized it because I didn't have Mom's recipe, and I lived in England, and calling her cost a fortune, we were poor as dirt, and she did not do email. So I had to make it up from memory. My ex-husband is a lasagna connoisseur and he adored this lasagna. Shh, don't tell him it's totally a cheat!*

Therefore, obviously, I had to give both versions to you.

Now...both Ryn and Boone suggest you eat their lasagnas with Ryn's mother's homemade Caesar salad. And just to say, if you haven't tried homemade, you... are...missing...OUT!

Ryn's Momma's Homemade Caesar Salad

2 stalks romaine lettuce, chopped

1 cup freshly grated Parmesan

6 slices bacon, cooked and crumbled

1 cup Butter Croutons (page 41)

Caesar Dressing

In a large bowl, combine all the ingredients and top with Caesar Dressing. Toss to coat.

*This recipe calls for the entire serving of dressing. If you prefer less dressing, add and toss to coat until your desired coverage.

CAESAR DRESSING

1 cup mayonnaise

½ cup grated Parmesan

Juice of 1 lemon (at least ¼ cup)

1 teaspoon Worcestershire sauce

1 teaspoon minced garlic

1 teaspoon anchovy paste

Combine all ingredients in a blender and blend for 2 minutes. Store in a Mason jar for up to 2 weeks.

Smoked Boston Butt

1 5-6 pound Boston butt

½ cup Auggie's BBQ Seasoning (page 105)

Coat the pork butt with the BBQ seasoning. Place the pork, fat side up, in a preheated 250 degree smoker for 10 hours, or until internal temperature reaches 190-200 degrees. During the smoking process, leave the smoker closed for the first 2 hours, then spray the butt each hour thereafter with apple cider vinegar. After the 10 hours, double wrap the butt in tin foil and place on smoker for an additional 2 hours. Remove from smoker, unwrap from foil and place on a large cutting board. Remove the pork bone and shred pork with 2 large forks.

Note: If you don't have a smoker, here's a crockpot version.

BOSTON BUTT (FOR PULLED PORK)

¼ cup apple juice

1 5-6 pound Boston butt

½ cup Auggie's BBQ Seasoning (page 105)

In a crockpot, place ¼ cup apple juice in the bottom of the pot. Rub the Boston butt with BBQ seasoning and place in crockpot. Cover and cook on low for 9 hours. Remove the Boston butt from the crockpot and discard all excess liquid. Remove the bone and shred meat while discarding any excess fat.

Filet with Blue Cheese Sauce

4 (1 ½-inch thick) filet mignons

Mag's Steak Seasoning (page 17)

4 tablespoons butter, softened

Blue Cheese Sauce

Preheat oven to 250 degrees. Rub the 4 filets generously with Mag's Steak Seasoning. Spread ½ tablespoon of softened butter on each side of the four filets. Allow to sit at room temperature for 10-15 minutes. In a large iron skillet over high heat, sear the 4 filets for 2 minutes on each side. Place in the oven for 8-10 minutes for medium rare. Remove from oven and top with 1 tablespoon of Blue Cheese Sauce.

BLUE CHEESE SAUCE

½ cup sour cream

½ cup mayonnaise

1 teaspoon Worcestershire sauce

1 teaspoon salt

1 teaspoon pepper

1 teaspoon garlic powder

¾ cup crumbled blue cheese

In a small bowl, combine all ingredients and refrigerate for at least 30 minutes before serving. Remove from refrigerator and allow to come to room temperature before topping on filet.

KA Note: Okay, this is another recipe I checked out in the RCL, and the steak seasoning is fab. But it's all about that blue cheese sauce. I think my eyes rolled back in my head the instant it hit my tongue. It's utterly superb.

Bacon Cinnamon Rolls

1 stick butter, softened

⅓ cup dark brown sugar

2 teaspoons cinnamon

1 package pizza dough

14 slices cooked bacon

⅓ cup maple syrup

2 cups powdered sugar

2 tablespoons milk

In a small bowl, mix together butter, brown sugar and cinnamon for filling. Roll out dough to ½-inch thickness to be about 9x13 in size. Spread filling evenly across dough. Cut into 7 even strips. Place 2 pieces of bacon on each strip and roll. Place all seven rolls in a greased 9-inch round pan. Bake on 350 for 35 minutes and remove from oven. Allow to cool for 10 minutes, then top with glaze. To make glaze, combine maple syrup, powdered sugar and milk until smooth.

Boone

Two weeks and six days before…

Boone moved into Ryn's living room with two loaded plates.

He did this announcing, "I get battle pay for cooking in that shitty-ass kitchen."

She burst out laughing.

Though, she wasn't so hysterical she couldn't take the food he offered.

Once he sat opposite her on her couch, he juggled his plate while extending napkin-wrapped utensils her way.

She reached across and took them, murmuring, "Thank you, baby." She then sat back saying, "You have no outdoor area at your pad, Boone. You can't smoke a pork butt for ten hours at your place."

"Your deck is only a half step up from your shitty-ass kitchen," he told her something she already knew. And he didn't quit bitching. "It's the size of a postage stamp and I gotta move that fucking cart you put in front of the back door out of the way just to access it."

"Poor pookie," she teased, shoveling shredded pork mixed with peach salsa in her mouth.

He tipped his head to her plate. "And the rest of that I made in your shitty-ass kitchen."

She caught his eyes, chewed, swallowed, and replied quietly, "I best get on designing your dream kitchen and making it a reality then."

Suddenly, he didn't give that first shit about cooking in her crappy kitchen.

"Yeah, sweetheart. You best get on that," he replied.

Her phone on the coffee table chimed and her eyes went to it.

"Speaking of," she said, leaning forward from where she was tucked up in the corner of the sofa with her food.

She grabbed her phone and sat back.

Using her thumb and face recognition, she read the text.

Then her gaze came back to him.

"Our counter to their counter was accepted," she announced. "They're going to send the paperwork. We have until tomorrow at five to sign."

Goddamn…

Brilliant.

Boone said nothing.

Ryn said nothing more.

They just looked at each other.

Eventually, she tossed her phone on the cushion between them and shared, "Axl's salsa is everything, but nothing beats your pulled pork, and as always, your Cobb is *da bomb*."

"Thanks, baby," he replied.

She went back to her plate, declaring, "Kitchen notwithstanding, I'm gonna miss this pad."

"You're not going to miss paying rent on it when you're at my place most of the time," he noted.

"True," she mumbled. Then louder, she said, "Totes gonna miss your pad too, though." She shot him a sassy smile. "We've had some fun there, baby."

"And we haven't had fun here?"

"There's more room there, and you have better equipment," she returned.

That was when he burst out laughing.

When he was done, the thought hit him.

They'd bought a house together.

No.

They'd already done that on her second flip.

They'd just bought *their* house.

"Rynnie," he whispered.

Her attention came right to him.

"I'll break my back to make you happy, honey," he vowed.

"I'll break mine so you won't have to," she returned.

Yeah.

That was his woman.

Her expression softened, her eyes hooded and her lips tipped up.

She then turned back to her plate.

Boone located the remote and hit go on their program.

And he settled in and watched something he wouldn't pick to watch, a Netflix documentary series about unsolved mysteries.

Ryn was addicted to that kind of stuff.

He wasn't a TV guy so he didn't care much either way.

The only thing he cared about was that, in the minimal downtime she allowed herself to have, she got to do something that chilled her out.

And for some reason, true crime chilled her out.

So he was good.

Though, regardless, he'd get to do what chilled him out later.

And he'd do it to Ryn.

His woman was addicted to that too.

KA

Jump ahead two weeks and six days...

"What's your favorite recipe?"

This time, I ask this question of Boone.

"Pulled pork," he answers.

"What's Ryn's?" I ask.

"The pulled pork. Always will be, no matter what I make."

That was definitive.

"Food and memories, hunh?" I note.

"Food and memories," he agrees.

I smile at him.

And Boone smiles back at me.

CHAPTER THREE

Comes from the Heart

KA

After Fortnum's...

We'd gotten sidetracked, repeatedly, mostly the guys handing each other shit, so the meeting went long before we could finish going over the recipes.

This meant they had to take off.

Though it was clear they liked me, considering they asked me to go to Auggie's house the next day to finish up.

Letting me into their space.

I was looking forward to it.

Aug was going to make pork rind nachos.

I was looking forward to that more.

This gave me time to do something there was no way in hell I wasn't going to do when I got to Denver.

I hit the castle up in the Highlands where High and Millie lived.

High, Millie, Poet...

And Chief.

The door to the huge silver boom mansion was opened before I even hit the steps up to the veranda.

High stood there.

It was incongruous, this handsome but very rough biker, standing in the doorway of a rather palatial, elegant Victorian home.

Still, I knew Millie.

So it totally worked.

When my foot fell on the veranda, I greeted, "Hey, High."

"Hey, babe," he greeted in return. But he waited until I stood in front of him before he said, "When I heard you were in town, knew you'd show."

Yeah.

Nothing could keep me away.

He stepped aside and I entered his house.

Even though I was scanning the floor as I did it, my attention was taken by movement as a man entered the room from a doorway to the left.

I looked into sapphire blue eyes I knew very well and said, "Hey, Tack."

His gravelly voice came softly.

He knew what this visit meant.

Tack always knew everything.

"Hey, darlin'."

That's when he bopped in, moving not with feline grace, but like a badger.

He'd never been graceful.

His sister wasn't either.

It was hilarious.

But now, as I took him in, my heart lurched.

Smooshed grumpy face.

Creamy thick fur with gray at his ears, on his tail and around his eyes, nose and mouth.

Ice-blue eyes.

My first Axl.

But in this world, he was known as Chief.

It's arguable, but that last might be a better moniker.

"Hey, Mr. Man," I said, bending as he made it to me.

I picked him up, cuddled him to my chest, bent my head to him, and he stared at my face with his intelligent eyes, putting his fluffy kitty paw to my mouth.

God, I'd forgotten how silky soft his fur was.

"Yeah," I whispered against his paw, "I miss you too."

Axl/Chief started purring.

A hand came to rest on the back of my neck, fingers curling around.

"Did good with his namesake, Kit," High said from beside me. "Man's solid. Treats his woman like gold."

"It's weird," I replied, still staring down at my kitten, "considering the inspiration."

Tack was now standing in front of me.

"Nothing's weird, babe," he stated. "Especially when it comes from the heart."

I looked up and again into his eyes.

"Red wants you for breakfast tomorrow," Tack declared. "I'm making pancakes. Can you hit the foothills in the morning?"

Tack, his wife Tyra (or as he called her, "Red") and Tack's pancakes?

There was only one answer to that.

"Absolutely."

CHAPTER FOUR

Take Care of You

Axl

Two weeks earlier...

Axl parked his Jeep next to the burgundy Murano that sat outside the converted storage units.

It was late.

It was dark.

And she wasn't responding to texts.

He was mildly relieved when he saw Hattie's Murano outside her unit.

But his woman replied to texts, that night he'd sent five, got nothing, so he wasn't totally relieved.

He exited his vehicle, went to the door to her unit, which was her studio, and as usual, didn't knock before he went in.

The space was as it always was: an organized mess that was only organized in a way Hattie understood.

And Hattie was in the middle of it, dust in her hair, streaks of it on her face, and her jeans-overall shorts and the tight tank she wore under were also covered.

Her gaze came right to him.

"I'm trying a new medium and it isn't working," she said irately, rather than saying something like, "Hey," or better than that, smiling at him, coming to him and offering her mouth.

He looked to the huge lump that sat on a thick wooden plank set over two sawhorses.

It, too, was covered in dust with added nuggets scattered around and overall coating of grit.

"It's a stone that's too porous. Everything I try, it crumbles."

She was still talking irritably.

"So move on," Axl suggested.

"But," her gaze strayed to the stone, "it's so pretty."

She was right.

Still.

"Babe," he said.

She was staring at the lump.

"Hattie," he called again.

She looked at him.

"I've texted you five times. No reply," he told her.

She looked shocked. "You have?"

Since she wasn't coming to him, he went to her.

And when he did, he caught her jaw gently in his hand and dipped his face to hers.

"Shit's been real in our crew, baby. I know you get into your thing when you're at your studio. But when I text, I need you to reply."

"Sorry, I got kinda involved," she muttered.

"Understandable," he said. "Just asking you to be mindful."

"I kinda don't even know where my phone is at this juncture," she admitted, and he grinned at her.

Yeah.

She could get involved when she created.

And her focus was sexy as fuck.

He still needed her to check in.

Especially now.

"I thought you were testing a recipe for that cookbook," she remarked.

"I was, and you were supposed to be there to taste it," he reminded her.

He dropped his hand from her jaw when she glanced around, saying, "I'll clean up a bit, we can go home, you can cook, and I can eat."

He stared at her a beat before he informed her, "Hattie, it's eleven o'clock at night."

Her eyes got huge. "It is?"

Too fucking cute.

He nodded.

"No way," she stated.

He chuckled and said, "Way."

"Whoa, think I got more than *kinda* involved."

"Yeah," he agreed, smiling down at her.

"So you were texting me to get my ass home so you could feed me?" she asked.

"Not exactly," he answered.

That was when she really took him in.

And after she did that, she leaned into him, putting her hands to his chest.

"What happened?" she asked quietly.

"Dad happened," he answered.

Her pretty face instantly went hard. "What'd he do?"

He didn't want to get into it there.

"Can we go home?" he requested.

She nodded immediately. "I'll just…dust off and we can get out of here."

"Thanks, baby."

She gave him a grin she didn't commit to considering her eyes were roaming his face, trying to get a bead on where he was at.

But she knew.

He was at where he always was when it came to his father.

Other than that, she didn't waste time "dusting off."

Then they were out of there, she locked up, got in her car, Axl pulled himself into his Jeep, and he followed her home.

 DREAM BITES COOKBOOK

An hour and a half later...

She was full-out on top of him.

It was after sex.

And after he'd shared.

"I kinda thought it was over, this crap with your dad," she said.

It would probably never be over.

That was the way family was.

Or at least that was the way his dad was.

"I don't have to respond," he told her.

"Are you going to respond?" she queried.

"No."

"I think that's a good call," she mumbled, her gaze wandering to his throat.

"He won't give up, though," he warned her, and she looked back to him.

"I know," she whispered sadly, watching him closely.

"Babe, I can hack it."

"Okay."

She didn't sound convinced.

So he repeated, "I can hack it."

Hattie lifted a hand, trailed her fingers across his cheekbone, and also repeated, "Okay." She then dipped her face closer and said, "Up for a second round tonight?"

Like she had to ask.

"My woman have creative energy to burn?"

"Frustrated energy," she amended, and his brows shot up, considering what they'd finished doing not fifteen ago.

And both of them definitely *finished.*

This made him ask, "How frustrated can you be?"

She giggled, dipped even lower, shoved her face in his neck, and whispered beneath his ear, "The creative part of frustrated, honey. Like normal, last time, you did all the work."

"If you're up for taking over, I'm not gonna stop you."

She lifted her head, gave him a grin, and kissed him.

After that, she kissed him a lot of other places.

But when she got between his legs, it wasn't about kissing.

It was about licking.

And sucking.

Hattie gave phenomenal head.

But he couldn't call it, whether he liked that better than when she took him to a place he couldn't hold back, and she got off huge getting her face fucked.

Which was what happened.

He'd had to take his knees, twine his fingers in her soft curls, and fuck her mouth while he watched her touch herself in front of him.

Christ, that ass.

Using her hair, as gently as he could in the state he was in, he pulled out and tipped her head back.

His voice was thick when he ordered, "Turn around, baby. On your belly. Legs tight together."

She was ready for him and he knew it when she scrambled to do as she was told and his cock jumped watching her do it.

He positioned, legs splayed wide, knees in the bed by her upper thighs, caught her hips in his hands, and found her, drilling deep into that slick wet.

"Fuck," he grunted.

She whimpered.

Hearing it, he grunted, "Fuck" again.

She squeezed his cock with her pussy.

Jesus.

Even if this was the second round, it wasn't going to last long.

"Hand under you, Hattie, baby, get yourself there," he demanded.

She shoved her hand under her, and he knew she hit the target when it brought another whimper.

Then she flipped her head so it was to the side rather than her forehead to the mattress and her dark curls flew all over his sheets.

Oh yeah.

This wasn't going to last long.

"Close?" he asked, his voice gruff.

"Honey," she gasped.

"Baby, you close?" he bit off.

"Axl," she sighed before her hips bucked, and her pussy pulsed around his cock.

Thank fuck.

He let go and joined her.

When he stopped coming, he had his head bowed and realized his fingers were digging into her flesh.

He relaxed, slid out, and came off his knees in order to lower himself and cover her back.

He shoved his face in the hair at her neck.

"You took over," she grumbled hazily.

He grinned.

"I was supposed to do all the work," she reminded him.

Axl lifted up only enough to pull her hair off her neck. He then kissed her there before he shifted to rest his cheek against her still-turned head.

"It didn't happen like that," he stated the obvious.

"It never happens like that. You always get all commando-y and take over."

He asked a question he knew the answer to.

"Is this a problem?"

"No, I just..." he felt her head move so he raised his as she twisted her neck and caught his eyes, "...wanted to take care of you."

Fuck.

He loved her.

"Baby," he murmured.

"But then you took care of me."

"Trust me, fucking your face then drilling you into the bed *totally* is taking care of me." He paused for emphasis and reiterated, "*Totally.*"

He felt her body move with her giggle.

So, smiling, he lifted up, turned her, then rested some of his weight on top of her, most of it into a forearm at her side.

And then he tangled his fingers into her curls and locked eyes.

"If I have you, I'm always okay."

"Axl—"

"It's the truth."

She framed his face in both hands.

"Sorry I missed Cooking with Axl tonight," she whispered.

"We'll do it tomorrow."

"'Kay."

He could hear she was getting sleepy.

So he bent, touched his mouth to hers, then murmured, "Let's get cleaned up so we can sleep."

"'Kay," she repeated.

He felt his face get soft before he rolled off, tugged her gently from the bed, and they headed to the bathroom.

The lights were out, and they were curled up together under the covers before she spoke again.

"I know I made it hard, but thank you for never giving up on me," she whispered.

He pulled her closer as he replied, "Hattie, baby, like I've told you before, you made it worth it."

She turned her head and kissed his collarbone.

"Love you," she said there.

"Love you too, now go to sleep."

"Bossy."

"Like you don't dig it."

"Arrogant."

"Like you don't dig that too."

"I'm shutting up now."

"Good call."

She let it sit a beat before she said, "Always the last word."

His body was shaking with his laughter even as he said a warning, "Hattie."

"Whatever," she mumbled.

She was dead to the world five minutes later.

It wasn't long before he joined her.

A S P

APPETIZERS

PETITE POTATO WEDGES WITH HOMEMADE KETCHUP

LOADED PETITE POTATO WEDGES

DEVILED EGGS 3 WAYS

PIMENTO CHEESE & BACON

MEXICAN STREET CORN

CAJUN CRAB

MAINS

TUSCAN CHICKEN

PORK TACOS WITH PEACH SALSA

APPLE STUFFED PORK CHOPS

DESSERTS

TURTLE PIE

COCA-COLA CAKE

DR. PEPPER CAKE

AXL'S APPETIZERS

Petite Potato Wedges with Homemade Ketchup

8 tablespoons (1 stick) butter, melted

12 petite red potatoes, cut into 4 wedges each

¼ cup all-purpose flour

¼ cup grated Parmesan cheese

1 teaspoon salt

½ teaspoon pepper

½ teaspoon garlic powder

Preheat oven to 350 degrees. Pour butter in a 9x13-inch baking dish. In a large bowl, combine remaining ingredients and toss to coat. Place each wedge on its side in the butter and bake for 30 minutes. Flip each potato to the other side and cook for an additional 20 minutes. Remove from oven and serve with Homemade Ketchup.

HOMEMADE KETCHUP

24 ounces tomato paste

½ cup brown sugar

½ cup honey

1 teaspoon garlic powder

1 teaspoon onion powder

½ teaspoon mustard powder

¼ teaspoon cinnamon

3 tablespoons Worcestershire sauce

½ cup apple cider vinegar

1 tablespoon salt

1 cup water

In a large saucepan over low heat, add tomato paste, brown sugar, and honey. Stir until sugar is melted. Bring to a low boil and add remaining ingredients. Simmer for 30 minutes, stirring every 1-2 minutes. Remove from heat and allow to cool completely. Place in a 32-ounce jar and refrigerate for up to 3 weeks.

KA Note: As of the writing of this book, I have not yet made this recipe. What I will say is, I'm dying to make homemade ketchup. I was in Sonoma at a fabulous restaurant with my good friend Danae, drinking amazing wine and eating amazing food, and the place had homemade ketchup. I told Suzanne this was my new culinary dream, to make my own ketchup. And as ever, Suzanne delivered.

Loaded Petite Potato Wedges

1 batch Cheese Sauce

¼ cup pickled jalapeño, diced

1 batch Petite Potato Wedges

6 slices bacon, cooked and crumbled

½ cup chopped green onion

½ cup Ranch Dressing

Prepare Cheese Sauce and add in the diced jalapeño. On a large platter, place Petite Potato Wedges in an even layer and top with Cheese Sauce. Top with bacon and green onion, then drizzle with Ranch Dressing.

CHEESE SAUCE

1 tablespoon butter

1 tablespoon all-purpose flour

¼ cup milk

1 (8 ounce) block Velveeta cheese

In a medium saucepan over low heat, melt butter and stir in flour to make a roux. Stir in milk until thickened, about 1-2 minutes. Add Velveeta to saucepan and stir until cheese is melted.

RANCH DRESSING

½ cup mayonnaise

¼ cup sour cream

2 tablespoons milk

¼ teaspoon dried chives

¼ teaspoon dried parsley

¼ teaspoon dried dill weed

¼ teaspoon garlic powder

¼ teaspoon onion powder

Pinch of salt and pepper

Place all ingredients in a mason jar and shake well. Refrigerate for up to a week.

Deviled Eggs 3 Ways

PIMENTO CHEESE & BACON

6 hard-boiled eggs

½ cup Auggie's Pimento Cheese (page 102)

4 slices bacon, crumbled

Slice eggs in half lengthwise and remove yolks. Place yolks in a small bowl and mash with a fork until all lumps are removed. Stir in the Pimento Cheese and fold in the bacon, reserving about 2 tablespoons for topping. Spoon into egg whites until cups are full. Top with remaining bacon and serve.

MEXICAN STREET CORN

6 hard-boiled eggs

¼ cup mayonnaise

1 tablespoon Dijon mustard

1 tablespoon Worcestershire sauce

½ teaspoon salt

½ teaspoon pepper

½ cup grilled corn

½ cup Cotija cheese

¼ cup green onion

1 tablespoon chili powder

2 tablespoons fresh cilantro, chopped

Slice eggs in half lengthwise and remove yolks. Place yolks in a small bowl and mash with a fork until all lumps are removed. Stir in mayonnaise, Dijon mustard, Worcestershire sauce, salt and pepper. Spoon into egg whites until cups are halfway full. Top evenly with grilled corn, Cotija cheese, green onion, chili powder, and cilantro to serve.

CAJUN CRAB

6 hard-boiled eggs

¼ cup mayonnaise

1 tablespoon fresh horseradish

1 tablespoon hot sauce

1 tablespoon Dijon mustard

¼ cup green onion

1 teaspoon Old Bay seasoning

¼ cup capers

½ cup lump crabmeat

¼ cup chopped chives

Slice eggs in half lengthwise and remove yolks. Place yolks in a small bowl and mash with a fork until all lumps are removed. Stir in mayonnaise, horseradish, hot sauce, Dijon mustard, green onion, and Old Bay seasoning. Then fold in capers and crabmeat. Spoon into egg whites until cups are full. Top with chives and serve.

KA Note: Growing up, deviled eggs were a staple starter at any summer get-together back home in Indiana. I loved them then. And as such, I wholeheartedly welcomed them back when they had their resurgence. And then some, because suddenly, they were gourmet.

So, suffice it to say, I was all in when Suzanne suggested deviled eggs for one of the boys to make for the cookbook. And I doubled down when Suzanne created these in her test kitchen for us. Each one, perfect bites of goodness. And not only because what Suzanne crafted is delicious, but because they remind me of home.

Tuscan Chicken

3 boneless, skinless chicken breasts

6 thin slices prosciutto

18 spinach leaves

6 ounces goat cheese

1 (8 ounce) jar sun-dried tomatoes, drained

4 tablespoons butter

2 tablespoons all-purpose flour

2 cups chicken broth

1 lemon

1 cup heavy cream

Preheat oven to 350 degrees. Cut each chicken breast in half. Place each half, one at a time into a resealable bag. Using a meat mallet or rolling pin, pound each chicken breast to ½-inch thickness. Lay each chicken breast flat. Place 1 slice of prosciutto, 3 spinach leaves, 1 ounce of goat cheese and 2 sun-dried tomatoes on top of the chicken. Roll each chicken breast and secure with a toothpick. In a large skillet over medium high heat, melt the butter. Add the chicken rolls and sear on each side for 2 minutes. Remove chicken from skillet and place on a cookie sheet. Bake chicken rolls for 15 minutes or until the internal temperature reaches 165 degrees. While the chicken is baking, using the same skillet, reduce the heat to low and add the flour. Using a wooden spoon, scrape all of the bits from the bottom of the skillet and stir to make a roux. Add in the chicken broth and stir until thickened. Add the juice of 1 lemon and the heavy cream. Continue to simmer for 1-2 minutes. Remove from heat. To serve, place chicken on a platter and top with lemon sauce.

KA Note: This was one of the recipes I tested myself in the RCL. Not only is this yumalicious, it's also easier to make than it looks, but it packs a serious punch in presentation. This is perfect for when you have company. And an added note, the sauce is insane. So freaking simple to make, so crazy good!

Pork Tacos with Peach Salsa

6 cups Smoked Boston Butt, shredded (page 49)

Vinegar BBQ Sauce

Peach Salsa

12 (6-inch) flour tortillas

In a large bowl, combine the pulled pork and Vinegar BBQ sauce. Place ½ cup of pulled pork on the center of a flour tortilla. Top with 2-3 tablespoons of peach salsa. Repeat with remaining 11 flour tortillas.

KA Note: If you have the time, and a smoker, make these tacos with Boone's Smoked Boston Butt (page 49). Though, when I made them, since I don't have a smoker, I made mine with a slow-cooked pork shoulder in my crockpot, slow cooking in the below BBQ sauce. Um...yum.

VINEGAR BBQ SAUCE

2 ½ cups white vinegar

¾ cup ketchup

¼ cup brown sugar

1 tablespoon salt

1 teaspoon pepper

1 teaspoon garlic powder

1 teaspoon onion powder

In a small pot over low heat, combine all ingredients and bring to a boil. Reduce heat to low and simmer for 10 minutes. Remove from heat, allow to cool and add to a mason jar. Store for up to 2 weeks in the refrigerator. Shake well before each use.

PEACH SALSA

6 fresh peaches, seed and skin removed, diced

½ cup sweet onion, diced

1 teaspoon minced garlic

1 fresh jalapeño, seeded and diced

½ bunch cilantro, finely chopped

1 teaspoon salt

1 teaspoon pepper

Juice of 1 lime

In a large bowl, combine all ingredients. Cover and refrigerate for 2 hours before serving. Store in refrigerator for up to 1 week.

KA Note: I'm not gonna lie. As noted above in my Monte Cristo babble, I'm not about adding sweet with savory. So when Suzanne put peach salsa with pork, my first thought was, "Euw." But if we did all the same things all the time, ate all the same things, listened to all the same music, etc., life would be super boring. So I gave it a go.

And...stop.

This peach salsa is the best salsa I have ever tasted in my life. And trust me, I've tested some salsa. Mixed with the pork, it's a taste explosion of such crazy goodness, it's mind boggling.

Making it better, the salsa keeps and it makes your refrigerator smell like fruity-spicy yumminess every time you open it. It's like a mini-fiesta whenever you need something from the fridge. Do yourself a favor and try this. You'll love it.

Apple Stuffed Pork Chops

2 tablespoons onion, chopped

3 tablespoons butter, softened

4 slices of bread, toasted and crumbled

2 cups finely chopped granny smith apple

½ teaspoon sage

½ teaspoon thyme

6 bone-in pork chops (1-inch thick)

1 teaspoon salt

1 teaspoon pepper

1 tablespoon oil

In a small skillet over medium heat, sauté onions in butter until tender. Remove from heat and add the bread crumbles, apples, sage and thyme. Cut a pocket in each chop by making a horizontal cut through the meat almost to the bone. Sprinkle inside and outside with salt and pepper and spoon stuffing loosely into pockets. In a large skillet over high heat, add oil and brown the chops on both sides for 2 minutes each. Place in an ungreased 9x13-inch baking dish. Cover with foil and bake at 350 degrees for 30 minutes. Uncover and bake 30 minutes longer or until a thermometer reads 145 degrees. Allow to rest for 5 minutes before serving.

Turtle Pie

1 cup light corn syrup

1 cup sugar

3 eggs

2 tablespoons melted butter

2 teaspoons vanilla extract

1 ½ cups crushed pecans

1 cup semi-sweet chocolate chips

1 deep-dish pie crust

Caramel Glaze

Preheat oven to 350 degrees. Mix together the corn syrup, sugar, eggs, butter, and vanilla until smooth. Add pecans and chocolate chips, then mix well. Pour into pie crust and bake for 1 hour. Remove from oven and drizzle with Caramel Glaze. Cool on wire rack for 1 hour before slicing.

CARAMEL GLAZE

4 tablespoons butter

½ cup brown sugar

½ cup heavy cream

¼ teaspoon salt

In a medium saucepan over medium heat, melt butter. Add the brown sugar and cook, stirring constantly for 1 minute. Add heavy cream and salt. Bring to a boil and continue cooking for 2 minutes. Remove from heat and cool for 15 minutes before drizzling over turtle pie.

Coca-Cola Cake

2 cups all-purpose flour

2 cups sugar

1 teaspoon baking soda

1 can Coca-Cola

2 sticks butter, melted

¼ cup cocoa powder

2 eggs

½ cup buttermilk

½ teaspoon vanilla extract

Chocolate Glaze

Preheat oven to 350 degrees. In a large bowl, whisk the first 3 ingredients until combined. In a small bowl, combine cola, melted butter and cocoa. Add to flour mixture, stirring just until blended well. Add in eggs, buttermilk and vanilla extract. Blend until combined, then pour into a 9x13-inch greased baking dish. Bake 25-30 minutes or until a toothpick inserted in center comes out clean. Remove from oven and pour Chocolate Glaze over hot cake. Allow to cool for 5-10 minutes before slicing.

CHOCOLATE GLAZE

½ cup Coca-Cola

1 stick butter, melted

¼ cup cocoa powder

4 cups powdered sugar

In a large bowl, whisk together the Coca-Cola, butter and cocoa. Next, add in the powdered sugar 1 cup at a time until everything is combined.

Dr. Pepper Cake

Suzanne Note: This cake came to be when, instead of Coca-Cola in the fridge, all I had was Dr. Pepper. It was an experiment that turned out AMAZING! To make this deliciousness, substitute Dr. Pepper for Coca-Cola and follow Coca-Cola Cake recipe.

KA Note to Suzanne's Note: I always giggle when I read that Suzanne used the word "deliciousness." No clue why, I used it too. But with Suzanne, it's damned cute.

CHAPTER FIVE

Messin' with Family

KA

Two weeks later...

After visiting with High, Tack, and my babies, I have dinner at Las Delicias with some friends.

This runs long, and I get a text in the middle of it.

A text that contains an order from someone I can't ignore, but even if I could, I wouldn't want to.

My plan is to head back to Hotel Teatro to get some shut-eye so I can get up early, have time to get gussied up, and caffeinate before I need to get on the road to drive into the foothills to have breakfast with Tack, Tyra and their boys.

But instead, I head to Colorado Boulevard.

Yeah.

I'm going to Smithie's.

I'm told my text from him will circumvent the velvet rope outside, and once I find a parking spot in the packed lot and head to the front door, I flash my phone screen to the bouncer and discover it does.

Under the baleful glare of the folks waiting in line, I'm ushered in, and with word from one bouncer to the other which ends with me being passed off from door bouncer to inside bouncer, I'm under escort.

In other words, I'm being marched to the staircase at the side of the strip club, beyond the bar.

A staircase that will lead me up to the office of the big man.

Smithie.

I want to dawdle, though I'm not given a choice.

Things are changing at Smithie's, and I've been hoping I could check it out.

Since that isn't an option, I take the option open for me and scan the space to see if I can find him.

I do.

Side wall, next to the door to the hall that leads to the bathrooms.

There's a fire exit at the end of that hall.

Jet staved off an attacker in that hall.

When Sadie was kidnapped, she was carried down that hall.

Now, Dorian "Ian" Walker, Smithie's nephew, the man Smithie was grooming to take over the club, has his wide shoulders to that wall.

Even in the darkened club, I can see the collared shirt he's wearing is pure class and pure quality.

I can also see his pecs bulging above his forearms crossed over his chest.

Hawt.

Ian isn't watching the stage.

He also doesn't have his eye on the crowd.

He's looking at me.

I give him a dorky wave.

He doesn't wave back.

He jerks up his chin.

Yeesh.

These guys.

Then I'm being led up some stairs.

When we make the top, the bouncer raps on the door three times… loudly.

"What?" I hear shouted from inside.

The bouncer opens the door and motions me in.

I go in.

Smithie is sitting behind his desk.

And he's scowling at me.

Well, hello to you too.

"What'd I do?" I ask as I move in,

The door closes behind me.

"Now, you're messin' with family," he states.

I stop behind one of the chairs in front of his desk and I'm irate.

"After all this time, are you saying you don't trust me?" I demand.

"He's my nephew," he tells me something I know very well.

"And?" I snap.

Smithie sits back in his chair and the litany begins.

"Girl, first time I met you, you were busting up my club."

I roll my eyes.

"This is *after* you had one of my waitresses threatened at knife point in my parking lot," he goes on.

"That wasn't my fault. That's on Ray," I remind him. "Well, not really. It's on Slick, but only because Ray fucked shit up."

"The place was a disaster after Eddie lost his mind on that bachelor party," Smithie recounts.

"What can I say?" I ask on a shrug. "Eddie's hotheaded."

"You roofied Sadie in my club," he reminds me.

"Well…" I say slowly, because that one was rough.

Though, it ended up pretty awesome.

"Do I have to remind you what you did to Daisy?"

I flinch.

That wasn't awesome at all.

"And the shit Ally got into here…*at my club*?" he presses on.

Yikes.

"Uh…"

"And for fuck's sake, woman, Lottie's stalker?" he clips.

"I will admit, he was serious gross," I mumble.

"And now you're eyeing *my nephew*?" he demands.

"Dorian's hot," I say in my defense.

"For fuck's sake," Smithie repeats in a mutter to the ceiling.

"And he's sweet. And a good listener. He's protective. And a smartass. And he's really sharp. Not to mention, he dresses *amazing*," I go on. "I mean, I can't *not* dream up something for him. Are you crazy?"

Smithie aims his eyes at me again and begs, "Please tell me she's a sister."

"Uh, *duh*," I reply.

He seems mollified by that.

Slightly.

"I'll tell you somethin' for nothin', I'm not looking forward to this," Smithie declares.

"Smithie, my friend, people wouldn't read it if it was boring," I point out.

"Seen movies with couples in boats, the dude's paddling, the woman sitting there with an umbrella, and he's reciting poetry. Women dig that shit."

I burst out laughing.

"I'm not joking," he says into my laughter.

I round the chair, sit in it, pull my shit together, and say, "Do you honestly want me to put Dorian in a boat and make him recite poetry?"

Smithie's lips hitch to the side.

"That's what I thought," I go on.

"Who's the woman?" he asks.

"I'm not saying," I don't answer.

"Is she a dancer?"

"No."

"Does he meet her at Fortnum's?"

"No."

"Is she a friend of Indy's?"

"No."

"Lottie's?"

"No."

"Daisy's?"

"No."

"Shirleen's?"

"No."

"Chaos?"

"No."

"Ally?"

I say nothing.

Smithie's eyes nearly bug out of his head.

There's more bass in his tone when he asks, "She's a private investigator?"

"Ummmmmmmmmmm..." I hum, drawing it out mostly because I sense he's about to lose it.

Smithie then loses it.

He shoots up out of his chair, shouting, "Holy fuck!"

"Smithie, relax, my man, she's not a private investigator."

"Then how does Ally know her?"

I try to look innocent and know I failed when Smithie asks, "Is she a cop?"

"Weeeelllll..."

He falls back into his chair, lands an elbow on the desk, and puts his head in his hand.

Yeah, he senses how much shit is going to go down.

Oh boy.

Smithie straightens on a snap and orders, "Don't shoot her."

"I—"

"Or shoot Ian."

"But—"

"Or kidnap her."

"Well—"

"Or Dorian."

"You see—"

"Or injure either of them in any way. Or fuck with their heads. Or—"

I cut him off this time.

"I can't promise that, Smithie. You know how it is. It happens, that being, they tell me their story, and I write it how it happens. And as you've learned, pretty much anything goes."

"At least tell me this, is she something else?"

I smile big at him.

"She's dynamite."

Smithie studies me for a long time.

Finally, he speaks.

"Are you ever gonna be done with us?" He asks this question on a heavy sigh.

"I hope not," I answer, meaning these words with my whole heart.

"If the results weren't worth the pain in the ass you are, you wouldn't leave this club," he totally lies.

"Don't try to feed me that, Smithie," I say, smiling at him. "I hate to break it to you, but you're a big softie and everyone knows it." I whirl my hand in the air indicating our current scene. "You don't fool anybody with this act."

"Yeah, not a big fan of you letting that cat out of the bag either," he returns.

I fight rolling my eyes again because that also isn't on me.

He totally sucks at hiding he's one of the best guys in the world.

He was the one who gave it to me.

I just wrote about it.

"Are you gonna offer me a drink and a VIP table or what?" I ask, deciding on the fly I could have just one, watch the show for a spell, and still be back to the hotel at a decent (ish) hour to get some rest in before I have to be up in the morning.

"French 75, Hendricks?" he asks back.

I smile at him. "You know me so well."

"You're a pain in my ass," he mutters as he rises from his chair.

"You still love me, though," I say as I rise from mine.

When he makes it to me, he slings his arm around my shoulders, I slide mine around his waist, and he guides me to the door, retorting, "Need to get my head examined, but yeah, I do."

And yeah.

I love coming home to Denver.

It rocks.

CHAPTER SIX

Something Special

KA

The next day, early afternoon …

I'm a little surprised I've been called to Axl's house.

The plan was late afternoon at Auggie's, pork rind nachos, Fat Tire beer, and swapping recipes and tales on his back patio.

So Axl texting me and asking me to his place before that happens is a surprise.

His house has no real yard, it's set just a bit off the sidewalk, and it's literally around the corner and down one single block from where I used to live in Denver's Baker Historical District.

It is, in fact, the house where I drank wine, ate food, shot the shit with my friends who lived there and babysat those friends' daughter.

A baby I sat with in my lap in the hall that was in the back of that house, running between bedrooms, and we made funny faces at each other in the closet door mirrors.

A baby that is now a grown woman who I attended her wedding who has her own baby.

Yeah.

Ugh.

Even if the exterior and location is my friends Dixie and Chris's old house, the interior is all Axl's.

It's da bomb.

After he invites me in, I look at the piece of art sitting on the cabinet in front of his window.

And the other piece in the corner.

I don't mention either as Axl invites me to take a seat on one of his couches, tells me we'll walk together to Auggie's as he lives just down the road, and then he excuses himself and heads to the kitchen.

When he returns, he has a couple of sheets of notepaper with him.

He sits next to me on the couch and says, "I wanted to give these to you to include in my section, but I didn't want to do it in front of the guys."

I think this is weird because we were talking about recipes.

I mean, why couldn't he share a couple of recipes in front of the guys?

I look down at the paper in my hand, and first think how classy it is he has monogrammed notepaper.

Then I flip from one to the other, and instantly, I know why he's not sharing these in front of the others.

I look back into his ice-blue eyes and whisper, "Axl."

"You didn't think I'd take care of you?" he asks.

Tears fill my eyes and then I'm in his arms.

"You knew I'd take care of you," he says in my ear.

"Yeah," I mumble against his shoulder.

"Yeah," he replies. "Something special."

He is so right.

Something special.

ASP

SANDWICH AND SIDE

FRIED PORK SANDWICH

FRIED CORN

AXL'S SANDWICH AND SIDE

Fried Pork Sandwich

(Kristen Ashley Favorite)

2 cups buttermilk

1 teaspoon salt

½ teaspoon pepper

½ teaspoon cayenne pepper

½ teaspoon garlic powder

4 thick pork loin boneless chops, butterflied and pounded thin

2 sleeves saltines

2 cups all-purpose flour

2 cups oil

½ cup mayonnaise

4 hamburger buns

12 dill pickle chips

In a 9x13-inch baking dish, stir together the buttermilk, salt, pepper, cayenne and garlic powder. Place the pork chops in the buttermilk, cover with plastic wrap and marinate overnight in the refrigerator. In a large resealable bag, add in saltines and flour. Close bag and pound with meat mallet or rolling pin until saltines are coarse crumbs. Heat oil in a large iron skillet over high heat to 365 degrees. Remove the pork from the buttermilk and dredge in the saltine crumbs. Fry two chops at a time in the oil until golden brown and internal temperature is 145 degrees. About 3 minutes per side. Remove from grease and drain on paper towels. Spread mayonnaise on each bun, top with 3 pickle chips each and fried pork. Enjoy!

 Full disclosure, Suzanne isn't just a fantastic cook, she's a friend. And somewhere in our conversations, I must have mentioned to her that this was my mother's favorite sandwich. It's a favorite of mine too. It's also an Indiana staple. I honestly haven't seen this anywhere else but in restaurants in Indiana. I crave it, and when I go home, I make certain to get one.

Never, as in never, when this was on a menu, did my mother pass it up.

When Suzanne sent the recipes for this cookbook, she'd added this as a gift to me.

As my mom has passed and I loved her beyond reason, obviously, this undid me.

Best. Gift. Ever.

And now, Suzanne, who never met my mom, and I get to give a little of my mom to you.

See?

Best.

Gift.

Ever.

Fried Corn

(Kristen's Version)

1 shit ton of butter

1 bag frozen corn

Salt and Pepper

If the world smiles on you, you own a cast iron skillet.

Get that puppy out.

If not, grab your normal skillet.

In it, dump the butter. I'd say start with a full stick (half cup). Have more ready. Get it melting on medium heat. Once that stick is nearly melted, pour in the bag of frozen corn. The whole bag. Frozen. Normally, I use yellow corn. Sometimes, when I'm feeling fancy, I use white. If the family's over, I use both because everyone eats the crap out of this (by everyone, that means my sister, brother, and me, because we grew up on it), so we need a lot of it.

Season with salt and pepper. Stir. Don't have the heat too hot, though you can go low if you want to keep this going while you do other things. Intermittently move the corn around the skillet. As the butter is absorbed and starts sticking to the pan, you might need to add in more globs.

No, this is not healthy. *At all.*

The end of this process is hotly debated. My sister, Erika, feels this is done when the corn has absorbed all the butter, is slick and shiny and cooked through. I, on the other hand, like the butter browned on the corn and the whole lot is a bit sticky and messy. Our brother, Gib, falls in between.

You do you.

KA Note: When I was growing up, our cast iron skillet never left the stove. We cooked everything in that. And fried corn, cheap as chips, was a delicacy. It's ridiculously delicious. Everyone in our family loved it. I know no other household on several continents that cooks corn this way. Anytime I introduce it to newbies, people think I'm mad. Probably because people aren't fans of courting impromptu, food-induced heart attacks.

Those people didn't grow up in Indiana.

When I pull myself together, Axl gets me a tissue. I wipe my face, hope my mascara isn't a disaster, and ask the inevitable questions.

"What's your favorite recipe?"

"Tuscan Chicken," he answers.

"What's Hattie's?" I ask.

"The Mexican Street Corn deviled eggs."

"Of course," I murmur, glancing away.

"I'm happy, babe," he says.

And I look back, right into Axl's ice-blue eyes.

"Forever and always, I'll be happy," he whispers.

It's trembling, but I smile at him.

And Axl, my Axl, smiles back at me.

CHAPTER SEVEN

All on My Side

KA

Forty-five minutes later…

In the time since being at Axl's to now, where I'm sitting on the brick, back patio at Auggie's house, I've discovered the worst.

My mascara was ruined during my crying jag.

Insult to injury, I didn't bring a tube for touch-ups.

But, who would ever think a commando would make me cry?

Okay, maybe that was stupid. I've found they do that to women, and not in bad ways.

Though (and not only because I have no choice), I prefer to focus on the good.

Pork rind nachos.

And the better.

Mo has joined us.

Mo is Lottie's man.

As mentioned, Lottie is Jet's sister.

And Jet is the Rock Chick whose story is told in the second Rock Chick book.

Are you getting how I can't let go of my people?

All the guys are tall.

Mag is very tall.

Mo is gargantuan.

He's also bald, built big, solid and tough, and has a mug many might think is frightening.

But I know his gentle soul.

So I know he's beautiful.

"I wanna hear about this private meeting between you and Kit," Auggie says to Axl.

"The operative word in that, the word that means you're not gonna hear shit, is 'private,'" Axl points out.

I say nothing, mostly because I'm shoving pork rind nachos into my gob.

Boone is studying Axl closely. "What needs to be private?"

"Do you men not understand the word 'private'?" Mag asks.

"We don't have any secrets between us," Boone states.

Mo grunts.

It's a grunt, but it says a lot.

Then again, Mo isn't a big talker, so those who know him can read a lot into the little he gives.

"You've got secrets?" Auggie asks Mo.

"Everyone has secrets," Axl says.

"I don't have any secrets," Auggie returns to Axl.

Mag coughs and the word "Bullshit," comes out when he does.

"Fuck off," Auggie shoots at Mag.

"I'll fuck off after you fuck off with being such a goddamn nose," Mag retorts.

Mo grunts again but this time a word is formed from it.

"Men."

They shut up.

God, but I dig these dudes.

Even if Mo has effectively ended it, I can see that Boone and Aug aren't big fans of not knowing what's going on with something in which they're involved.

So I wade in.

"Uh, you boys *do* know that you'll find out what happened with Axl and me when the book is published."

"I'm not reading this book," Auggie says.

"Me either," Mag adds.

"Nope," Boone puts in.

"Negatory," Axl finishes it.

Um.

Excuse me?

"But...why?" I ask.

They all just stare at me.

Mo lifts a big mitt, reaches out to me and squeezes my shoulder.

"Don't worry, babe, I'm *totally* gonna read it," he says.

I shoot him a smile. "Thanks, Mo."

On this, the back door to Auggie's duplex (which I have recently discovered is *my* duplex, a duplex I gave to Indy for her book and a duplex Indy and Lee sold to Auggie recently) opens and a Black woman in a V-necked, body-hugging dress of orange and white stripes that run this way and that, steps out.

She does this on a pair of fabulous, spike-heeled orange strappy sandals.

And she does it carrying a scrapbook.

Nope.

The scrapbook.

"Did I not make it clear when the pork rinds come out, a phone call is made to me?" Elvira, Hawk's office manager and general chick-you-wanna-know demands.

She then clicks and clacks to Auggie's outdoor table and drops Tod's Wedding Planner Scrapbook on it.

"You left this at Fortnum's," she announces to Mag.

"Well, that tactic didn't work," Axl says to Mag under his breath.

"No, it didn't," Elvira agrees. "And pullin' that shit, I had a chance to peruse. I made notes for Evie. My stickies are the ones shaped like a star." After delivering that, she turns to me. "Hey, girl."

"Uh, hey," I reply.

"You the cookbook queen?" she asks.

"Well, no. Suzanne, my partner in this project, is. I'm just writing the narrative."

"Mm-hmm," she hums then turns to Auggie and notes, "I'm still standing."

"Vira, this is our thing with Kit," Auggie replies.

Elvira says nothing, she just holds his gaze.

"For fuck's sake," Auggie says, getting up, offering his chair to her, and then prowling off, presumably to find another seat for himself.

He does this heading to the house, so Elvira takes that opportunity to seat herself at the same time shouting, "I eat these nachos, I'll need a drink. And I am eating these nachos."

"On it," Aug says, waving his hand in the air and not looking back as he enters his home.

Elvira reaches for a pork rind, asking me, "This gonna be a steamy cookbook?"

"So far, yes," I tell her.

A variety of heavy sighs sound from around me.

But Mo chuckles again.

"Got no choice with these boys," she mumbles. "All testosterone and gunpowder."

Another chuckle from Mo.

And another sigh from Boone.

"Who are we up to?" she asks.

"We were about to get into Auggie," I say.

She munches her nacho, swallows, and replies, "Perfect timing, then. Also, don't let me leave without giving you instructions on one of my boards."

Oh.

My.

Gawd.

"Seriously?" I ask.

"Seriously," she answers.

I lean toward her and breathe, "I would *love* that."

She shrugs. "No problem, babe. Got it all ready for you."

And she reaches for another nacho.

Auggie

One week earlier…

When his woman walked into his kitchen, her eyes were sleepy but warm, and they were doing a thing they did often when she discovered them together.

They were losing the battle to take in her daughter and her man all at the same time.

She was up from a nap because she always ran herself ragged.

But she was also a mother, so she didn't stay hazy for long.

And this time was no exception.

"What on earth?" she asked.

"Momma!" Juno cried, whirling from the counter where they were just finishing up what was in the pan. "Auggie and me are making Chocolate Butter Bars!"

"I see that," Pepper murmured as she walked to them. "And it kinda scares me."

"It shouldn't," Juno returned. "Auggie and me dreamed it up, ran to the store and got all the goods, came back, put it together, and *I know* when it's all baked it…is gonna…be…*yum*."

Aug watched as she slid her arm around her daughter's shoulders, bent to kiss the top of Juno's hair, and said there, "Looks like it can't not be."

Juno tipped her head back to look up at her mother.

"I know, right? Sugar cookie dough, brownies and *Nutter Butters*. I mean, *whaaaaaaaat*?"

Pepper smiled at her girl.

Aug's heart squeezed.

"Gotta put these in, honey," he broke into their convo. "You wanna do it, or you want me to?"

"I'll do it!" Juno said excitedly.

"Right, oven's ready," he told her.

Juno broke from her mom, grabbed the pan, and even though she wasn't too young, she also wasn't very old, so both Aug and Pepper watched closely as she carefully slid it in the oven.

Once she closed the door, she whirled on them and declared, "Thirty-five minutes and then...*ecstasy.*"

Pepper laughed.

Auggie chuckled.

"Will you set your phone, Auggie?" Juno asked.

"Definitely, sweetheart," Aug answered, reaching to the counter to nab it.

"Since you're not on the couch anymore, I'm gonna go watch TV. Is that okay, Momma?" Juno queried.

That didn't make Aug's heart squeeze.

It made his gut tense.

"Sure, baby," Pepper said softly.

"Cool," Juno replied, then she was off.

She was a good kid. Sweet. Polite. Funny. Respectful. Full of personality.

But she was careful.

Too careful.

And the polite and respectful she often took to extremes.

That was about her shitheel of a dad.

And maybe the lunatics that made up the rest of Pepper's family.

"It's okay, she's back with us, she'll settle in."

Auggie stopped looking at the door Juno disappeared through and turned his attention to his woman.

"It pisses me off," he told her something she already knew.

"I know," she confirmed. "Set your timer, baby."

He looked down, engaged his phone, and set the timer.

When he was done, he had both of Pepper's arms around his middle with her pressing up against him.

So he slid an arm around her shoulders.

Christ, she smelled good.

He looked into her face.

And fuck, she was gorgeous.

"She's back with us," she repeated softly. "And she can be herself with me and you. Just Juno. All Juno. You give her that, Auggie. She's safe here and she knows it. And that's not only the best we can do, it means a lot to Juno."

That didn't make it piss him off any less.

But he didn't share that.

He said, "Yeah."

She pressed closer. "Thank you for giving that to my girl, baby."

He squeezed her around her shoulders as he engaged his other arm to curl it around her back, using both to pull her even closer.

"It's me who should be thanking you."

She smiled up at him, some of the sleep still in her eyes, the warmth definitely there, but magnified.

"When we make our babies, Auggie, you'll understand. I love you said that, but with what you give my baby, the gratitude is all on my side."

Pretty much everything she said meant he had no choice.

So he bent his head and kissed her.

Hard and wet.

APPETIZERS

PIMENTO CHEESE HUSHPUPPIES
WITH BLUEBERRY PEPPER JELLY

1-2-3-GO PORK RIND BBQ NACHOS

1-2-3-GO PORK RIND FIESTA NACHOS

MAINS

CHICKEN GYROS

"PRE-GAME" PHILLY CHEESE RIBEYE STEAK

HAM AND HASH CASSEROLE

DESSERTS

CANDIED CASHEWS

AUGGIE AND JUNO'S
CHOCOLATE BUTTER BARS

AUGGIE'S APPETIZERS

Pimento Cheese Hushpuppies with Blueberry Pepper Jelly

1 (8 ounce) package hushpuppy mix

¼ cup diced onion

¾ cup milk

½ cup Pimento Cheese

oil for frying

In a medium bowl, combine hushpuppy mix, onions, and milk. Allow to sit for 10 minutes, then stir in Pimento Cheese. Drop the batter, in tablespoon-sized balls, into oil that has been heated to 350 degrees. Fry for 1 minute on each side. Drain on paper towels. Serve with Blueberry Pepper Jelly.

PIMENTO CHEESE

1 (4 ounce) jar pimentos, not drained

8 ounces shredded sharp cheddar (yellow)

8 ounces shredded sharp cheddar (white)

1 tablespoon garlic powder

1 cup mayonnaise

Mix all ingredients and refrigerate for at least an hour before serving.

BLUEBERRY PEPPER JELLY

2 cups fresh jalapeños, pureed

2 cups fresh blueberries

5 cups sugar

1 cup apple cider vinegar

1 (3 ounce) pouch liquid pectin

12 (4 ounce) jelly jars or 6 (8 ounce) jelly jars

In a large saucepan, mix first four ingredients together and bring to a rolling boil. Allow to boil for 10 minutes. While the mixture is still boiling, add the liquid pectin and stir continuously for 1 minute. Then, ladle the mixture into the jelly jars, leaving ½ inch headspace. Apply caps and let jelly stand in refrigerator until set, about 12 hours, or transfer to a pressure cooker to seal for a longer shelf life. If you are not using a pressure cooker to seal the jars, the jam must stay refrigerated. Refrigerated jams are good for about 3 months. Sealed jars have a shelf life of about 18 months to two years.

KA Note: My first introduction to Suzanne—the person and her cooking—was at a 1,001 Dark Nights party at an industry event in Atlanta. And that introduction was Suzanne's pepper jelly.

Suffice it to say, I parked my ass close to the platter with this jelly, cheese and crackers and didn't move for a good long while.

That was several years ago.

To this day, I do not exist without more than one jar of this jelly (just pepper, or blueberry and pepper, or whatever she dreams up to add to the pepper) in my cupboard. I use it for a recipe Suzanne gave me that we'll include below with Elvira's board. I use it for a recipe from Suzanne and Lexi Blake's Master Bits and Mercenary Bites cookbook. And I panic if I start to run low.

I might learn one day not to panic.

Suzanne always takes care of me.

1-2-3-GO Pork Rind BBQ Nachos

6 cups oil for frying

1 cup pork rind pellets

1 tablespoon BBQ Seasoning

1 cup Axl's Cheese Sauce (page 68)

½ cup Alabama White Sauce

¼ cup sweet onion, diced

1 cup Boone's Smoked Boston Butt, shredded (page 49)

In a large Dutch oven or deep fryer, bring oil to 350 degrees. Drop 1-12 pellets into the oil and hold down in oil for one minute using a large slotted spoon. The pellets will triple in size. Drain on paper towels, then place them in a paper bag. Sprinkle in BBQ Seasoning. Close the bag and shake! Place on a platter and top with Cheese Sauce, Alabama White Sauce, onions, and Smoked Boston Butt.

BBQ SEASONING

2 tablespoons salt

1 tablespoon cumin

1 tablespoon paprika

1 tablespoon garlic powder

1 tablespoon onion powder

1 tablespoon chili powder

1 tablespoon brown sugar

1 tablespoon black pepper

1 teaspoon cayenne pepper

Combine all ingredients in a small bowl. Place in a (4 ounce) mason jar and store, unrefrigerated, for up to 3 weeks.

ALABAMA WHITE SAUCE

2 cups mayonnaise

½ cup apple cider vinegar

¼ cup hot horseradish

2 tablespoons lemon juice

2 teaspoons mustard

1 teaspoon black pepper

1 teaspoon salt

½ teaspoon cayenne pepper

½ teaspoon garlic powder

Place all ingredients in a medium bowl. Whisk thoroughly until creamy and smooth. Cover and refrigerate until ready to use.

1-2-3-GO Pork Rind Fiesta Nachos

1 pound ground beef

¼ cup plus 1 tablespoon taco seasoning

6 cups oil for frying

1 cup pork rind pellets

Axl's Cheese Sauce (page 68)

½ cup Avocado Dipping Sauce

1 cup pico de gallo

In a medium skillet over medium heat, brown ground beef. Drain and return to skillet. Add in ¼ cup of taco seasoning with ½ cup of water. Simmer for 10 minutes, then remove from heat. In a large Dutch oven or deep fryer, bring oil to 350 degrees. Drop 1-12 pork rind pellets into grease and hold down in oil for one minute using a large slotted spoon. They will triple in size. Drain on paper towels, then place in a paper bag. Sprinkle 1 tablespoon of taco seasoning into the bag, then close and shake! Place pellets on a platter and top with Cheese Sauce, seasoned ground beef, Avocado Dipping Sauce, and pico de gallo.

AVOCADO DIPPING SAUCE

2 avocados, halved and pitted

½ cup Greek yogurt

1 teaspoon minced garlic

½ teaspoon salt

Juice of 1 lime

Add all ingredients to a stand-up mixer and blend on low for 1 minute.

 As of publication, even though this was the first recipe I wanted to try, by the time I got into checking out the ones that I hadn't tasted in the test kitchen, the COVID-19 pandemic had struck so I didn't have the opportunity to find pork rind pellets.

But I'm gonna. Definitely.

And I. Can't. Wait.

Chicken Gyros

8 boneless, skinless chicken thighs

16 ounces Greek yogurt

1 tablespoon salt

1 tablespoon coriander

1 tablespoon cumin

1 teaspoon cayenne pepper

1 teaspoon cinnamon

1 teaspoon black pepper

¼ cup oil

1 tablespoon minced garlic

Juice of 1 lemon

1 onion, cut in half

2-3 wooden skewers

8 flour tortillas

Shredded lettuce

Diced tomatoes

Diced onions

Tzatziki Sauce

Place chicken thighs in a large bowl. Combine the yogurt, salt, coriander, cumin, cayenne, cinnamon, black pepper, oil, garlic, and lemon juice in a small bowl and pour over chicken. Cover with plastic wrap and refrigerate for 24 hours. Preheat oven to 400 degrees. On a foil-lined cookie sheet, place one onion half cut side down in the center of the sheet. Place 2-3 skewers in the center of the onion. Thread each chicken thigh, covered in marinade, onto the skewers, making a tower. Place in the oven and bake for 1 hour and 45 minutes to 2 hours or until a meat thermometer reads 165 degrees. Remove from oven and allow to rest for 10 minutes before slicing. Using an electric knife, thinly slice the chicken, starting at the top of the tower and working your way down. Place about ½ cup of sliced chicken onto a flour tortilla and top with shredded lettuce, diced tomatoes and diced onion. Drizzle with desired amount of Tzatziki Sauce.

TZATZIKI SAUCE

1 cucumber

1 cup plain Greek yogurt

1 tablespoon minced garlic

1 tablespoon red wine vinegar

1 tablespoon fresh dill, minced

¼ teaspoon salt

¼ teaspoon pepper

Remove the skin from the cucumber and cut in half lengthwise. Scrape out seeds and grate the cucumber. Place the grated cucumber on a cheese cloth and squeeze out all excess liquid. In a medium bowl, combine the cucumber with the remaining ingredients. Mix well, cover and refrigerate for 24 hours.

Pre-Game Philly Cheese Ribeye Steak

2 (8-10 ounce) ribeye steaks

2 tablespoons Mag's Steak Seasoning (page 17)

1 onion, thinly sliced

10-12 button mushrooms, thinly sliced

3 tablespoons soy sauce

5 tablespoons butter, divided

6 hoagie rolls, sliced in half

½ cup mayonnaise

12 slices provolone cheese

Preheat grill to 350 degrees. Spread the Steak Seasoning evenly over the 2 steaks. Allow the steaks to marinate and reach room temperature, about 30 minutes. While steaks are marinating, turn one side of the grill to high heat. Sear the steaks on each side for 2 minutes. Remove from high heat and place on the other side of the grill for the remaining grill time of 8-10 minutes or until the internal temperature reaches 145 degrees for medium rare. Remove from the grill and tent with foil. Allow to rest for 10 minutes before thinly slicing. In a medium skillet over medium heat, melt 2 tablespoons of the butter and add in sliced onion and mushrooms. Pour soy sauce over vegetables and stir to combine. Sauté for 10-12 minutes or until vegetables are tender. Preheat oven to 375 degrees. Spread remaining butter onto each side of the hoagie rolls and place in the oven for 3-5 minutes to toast the bread. Remove from oven and spread one side of each roll with mayonnaise. Place 5-7 steak slices, ¼ cup sautéed vegetables, and 2 slices of provolone cheese onto each roll. Place all the rolls on a cookie sheet and return to the oven for 5 minutes. Serve immediately or wrap individually in foil and pack in a cooler to keep warm until the pre-game.

Ham and Hash Casserole

2 cups chopped ham

1 (32 ounce) bag frozen hash browns

2 cans cream of potato soup

8 ounces sour cream

1 cup shredded cheddar cheese

1 cup shredded Parmesan

4 ounces cream cheese

½ cup chopped green onion

1 teaspoon salt

1 teaspoon pepper

Preheat oven to 350 degrees. In a large mixing bowl, combine all ingredients. Place in a greased 9x13-inch baking dish. Bake for 1 hour and 15 minutes.

Candied Cashews

1 egg white

1 tablespoon water

1 pound cashews

½ cup brown sugar

1 teaspoon cinnamon

1 teaspoon nutmeg

1 teaspoon vanilla extract

Preheat oven to 250 degrees. Using a hand mixer, combine the egg white and water until foamy. Stir in remaining ingredients until cashews are coated evenly. Spread onto greased cookie sheet and bake for 1 hour, stirring halfway through.

Auggie and Juno's Chocolate Butter Bars

1 tube sugar cookie dough

1 container Nutter Butter® cookies

1 box brownie mix

2 eggs

½ cup oil

Preheat oven to 350 degrees. In a greased 9x13-inch baking dish, spread cookie dough to cover entire bottom surface. Then lay Nutter Butter® cookies evenly across the cookie dough. In a large bowl, mix together the brownie mix, eggs, oil and ¼ cup water. Pour over cookies and spread to evenly cover entire dish. Bake for 35-40 minutes or until a toothpick inserted in the middle comes out clean.

KA Warning: Suzanne made these for us. As you prepare them, multi-task by girding your loins. Once these come out, and you try them, you'll lose your goddamn mind and want to shove your face in the pan. Be kind. Share. Or be smart. Pace yourself. Or be smarter. Make sure you have the ingredients for more than one batch.

Bonus Round

an Elvira Board

Hot Pepper Brie in Puff Pastry

♡ my Famous Cosmopolitan

An Elvira Board

1 jar garlic- or blue cheese stuffed olives (or both)

1 jar cornichons

1 wedge Jarlsberg cheese, cubed

1 container roasted red peppers

1 jar/container Marcona or Valencia almonds, salted

1 bag/container of salted cashews and/or Auggie's Candied Cashews (page 112)

Packages of Board Crafter's Choice:

Slices of Spanish chorizo, prosciutto, salami and/or Soppressata.

1 apple (sliced medium thin)

Bunches of red and green grapes, washed

1 basket strawberries, washed

1 jar fig spread

1 jar whole grain mustard

Assorted Crackers and Sliced Breads

1 pan Auggie and Juno's Chocolate Butter Bars (page 113) cut in small squares and/or

1 batch Evie's Cinnamon Clusters (page 22)

1 Hot Pepper Brie in Puf Pastry

Arrange all ingredients on a very large plate, platter, tray or board in an artful matter with small bowls for the olives, cornichons, spread and mustard.

Slap anyone's hand who's around who dares touch it before you're ready for the grand presentation.

This is no joke on the quantity side, so make it for four or more people.

Hot Pepper Brie in Puff Pastry

1 sheet frozen puff pastry, thawed

1 round Brie

1 (4 ounce) jar Pepper Jelly, or you can use Auggie's Blueberry Pepper Jelly (page 103)

1 egg

Heat the oven to 400 degrees. Unfold the pastry sheet and place the cheese in the center. Spread the jar of pepper jelly on top of the cheese and fold the pastry up and over the cheese to cover. Press to seal the seams. Beat the egg and 1 tablespoon of water in a small bowl with a fork or whisk. Place the pastry seam side down onto a greased baking sheet. Brush the top with the egg mixture and bake for 25 minutes or until pastry is golden brown.

PEPPER JELLY

2 cups pureed hot peppers (jalapeño and cayenne)

2 cups pureed bell peppers (green, red or yellow)

5 cups of sugar

1 cup apple cider vinegar

1 pouch liquid pectin

12 (4 ounce) jelly jars or 6 (8 ounce) jelly jars

Red or Green food coloring (optional)

In a large saucepan mix first four ingredients together and bring to a roaring boil. Allow to boil for 10 minutes. While the mixture is still boiling, add the liquid pectin and stir continuously for 1 minute. Then ladle the mixture into your jars, leaving ½ inch headspace. Apply caps and let jelly stand in refrigerator until set, about 12 hours, or transfer to your pressure cooker to seal for a longer shelf life. If you are not using a pressure cooker to seal the jars the jam must stay refrigerated. Refrigerated jams are good for about 3 months. Sealed jars have a shelf life of about 18 months to two years.

KA Note: Since discovering Suzanne's pepper jelly, and after she sent me some recipes, I have made this Brie in Puff Pastry countless times. It's my go-to appetizer for when I have company. And even my most health-conscious friends have thrown their healthy-living mojo out of the window to devour this without thought, willpower or remorse. It is the perfect combination of decadence.

Topping that, when you serve it, it makes you look like a culinary queen, which you will be, of course, if you make the whole of it. But I'm not, since I cheat due to Suzanne being my Pepper Jelly Dealer.

Elvira's Famous Cosmopolitan

Cirôc vodka

Cranberry juice

Cointreau

Fresh lime juice (or bottled, in a pinch)

Orange, lemon or lime rind for twist

Chill martini or coupe champagne glasses in the freezer for no less than 10 minutes.

Fill cocktail shaker with ice.

For each drink to be served, add two shots vodka, 1 shot cranberry juice, and ½ -to-¾ shot each of lime juice and Cointreau.

Shake vigorously in the shaker and strain into chilled glasses. Garnish with citrus twist.

Mixologist's option: Go the "Full Elvira" and purchase a Dior tote bag and travel sizes of all the above so it can be mixed at your whim wherever you are.

 DREAM BITES COOKBOOK

KA

Fast forward one week...

I excuse myself from the patio and meet Auggie in his kitchen.

He's making Elvira a Cosmo, so it's clear she's no stranger to Auggie's pad, because Aug is not a Cosmo type of guy, but all the ingredients are there.

I get close to him and offer, "Can I help?"

"You can grab some fresh Fat Tires from the fridge," he says.

I do that and come back to him as he's straining Elvira's drink into a glass.

"I'm sorry," I say low. "I haven't gotten to writing yours and Pepper's..."

"It's okay," he says softly.

"This means your part in the cookbook is gonna be small," I warn.

"It's okay," he repeats, turns, and shoots a white smile at me. "Save the best for last, yeah?"

I nod, my lips curving, and reply, "Yeah." I give it a beat and ask, "What's your favorite recipe?"

"Totally the Philly Cheese," he answers.

"What's Pepper's?"

"Those candied cashews are all for my woman."

As it should be with a Next Gen Rock Chick.

"And Juno's?" I press on.

"Chocolate Butter Bars, for certain."

No surprise there.

"You're a good man, Auggie," I tell him.

He smiles again at me.

And I smile back.

CHAPTER EIGHT

KA

Three and a half hours later...

You aren't going to believe this.

Or maybe you are.

I've been kidnapped.

One second, exiting my Lyft outside Hotel Teatro...

The next, I have a hood over my head, my hands are being zip-tied behind me and then I'm shoved in the backseat of a car.

We're on our way before the driver asks, "It's a long ride, got a preference for music?"

"The hood is unnecessary. I know who you are, Sly, and I know where we're going," I reply.

"Elvis Costello's Greatest Hits it is," he mutters.

I refuse to give him points for good taste.

"Pump It Up" comes on and I experience pain at the effort it takes not to sing along and rock to the beat.

Stupid Sly.

He's not wrong, the ride is long.

And after it's over, I'm hauled out of the back of the car.

It's colder there than it is in the city.

I'm shuffled somewhere that's warm and smells of piñon.

The ties are cut from my wrists, I'm pushed into a chair (that I will *not* admit is very comfortable) and the hood is pulled off.

I feel my hair fly and see I'm in a fabulous, elegant, welcoming, large mountain-house living room.

A fire is crackling in the fireplace beside me.

And Brett "Cisco" Rappaport is sitting in an armchair opposite me.

"Are you kidding me with this?" I demand as I irately smooth my hair.

"You come to town, you don't contact me?" Brett replies. "I'm hurt."

"I've been busy, Brett."

"Not so busy you haven't spent quite a bit of time with Magnusson, Sadler, Pantera, and Hero."

Uh…

Seriously?

"Have you been following me?"

He ignores my question and carries on.

"And Tack, High, and Smithie."

The dude is totally following me.

"Um, Brett—"

"And your plane leaves tomorrow morning, first thing."

"It does not," I refute. "I don't do anything first thing in the morning when I'm not writing. That's Kit's Lazy Make Up Stories in Her Head Time which intermittently mingles with Starla Deigning to Cuddle with Me Time."

"I'll amend," Brett offers. "Your plane leaves tomorrow, first thing as defined by what you consider first thing after lazy time."

I roll my eyes before I retort, "I have a cookbook to write."

"To raise money for women's charities. And I'm not on your call list?"

Regrettably, he has a point.

"I've been dealing with hella whiplash of nostalgia, resurgent sorrow and hot guy overload, cut me some slack," I demand.

"This is an emerging theme, Kit," he informs me. "I'm always coming up empty."

"I don't know what to say, bruh. Except I got something saved up for you and epicness doesn't happen," I lift a hand and snap my fingers, "just like that."

"Epicness?"

"Please," I scoff. "Like I'm not gonna take care of you."

His smile is slow.

And it's cute.

And hot.

Lord help me.

"I've got some recipes for you," he states.

My outlook brightens. "Really?"

"Of course." He turns his head and looks around the wing of his wingback.

Sly reads this cue and walks out of the room.

While he's gone, I note to Brett, "Zip ties and hood, bro. Overkill."

"I wanted your attention."

"Well, you got it."

"And there, you see, my strategy was successful."

"You could have just called and said, 'Hey, come on over. I'll start a fire and make hot chocolate. If you need a ride, I'll send Sly.'"

"I don't have any hot chocolate."

"Well, thanks. Now I know what to get you for Christmas."

While Brett chuckles low, Sly returns carrying some papers.

He hands these to me.

"Thanks," I mutter as I take them, then I look through them. "Dude," I say to the papers before I lift my head and look again at Brett. "These are choice."

"I'm hardly going to give you shitty recipes."

I look back down at the papers, telling him, "This is cover material."

"Well then, that makes me feel better."

Once more, I give him my attention and I do this to smile.

He smiles back.

When this happens, the doorbell rings.

Brett tenses.

I watch Sly walk out of the room.

"Expecting company?" I ask Brett.

"No," he answers.

Fabulous.

I hope this doesn't mean imminent firefight.

What?

I'm not being dramatic.

It's happened.

Not a minute later, in strolls Hawk Delgado, Sly on his heels.

"For fuck's sake," Brett sighs on sight of Hawk.

"That's my line," Hawk returns, then, to me, "Kit, out in the car."

"You're not the boss of me," I retort.

Hawk levels his eyes at me. "Kit. Out. In. The. Car."

"Okeydoke," I mutter, get up from my chair, and start to scoot. But as I pass Brett, I say, "Later, dude. Thanks for the recipes."

"Later, sweetheart," he bids. "And you're welcome."

And as I pass Sly, I say, "Pump it up, brother."

"Word," he replies.

APPETIZER

Grilled Cheese Bread Bowl
with Tomato Basil Soup

MAINS

Oh' Honey, You're Hot!...
Chicken Sandwich

Nashville Hot Chicken

DESSERTS

Key Lime Cream Pie

Brownie Lasagna

Chocolate Chess Pie

BRETT'S APPETIZER

(Or Main as this is soup, but also so much more!)

Grilled Cheese Bread Bowl with Tomato Basil Soup

1 sourdough bread bowl

8-10 deli slices extra sharp cheddar cheese

8-10 deli slices swiss cheese

1 stick butter, melted

1 teaspoon garlic powder

1 teaspoon chopped parsley

Preheat oven to 400 degrees. Cut a hole in the center of the bread bowl about 3 inches in diameter. Dig out all of the bread but not going through the bottom. That is your soup vessel. Cut a 1-inch deep cut around the entire bowl just below the middle circle. Repeat about 2 inches lower with the same cut. Stuff the cheese slices in every little slit of bread and lay flat in the center bowl and around the sides. In a small bowl, mix together the butter, garlic powder and parsley. Brush over the entire bread bowl to cover. Bake for 8-10 minutes or until golden and bubbly. Add about 1-2 cups of tomato basil soup, depending on the size of the bread bowl.

TOMATO BASIL SOUP

2 (28 ounce) cans San Marzano tomatoes, whole

3 tablespoons olive oil

1 Vidalia onion, finely diced

1 teaspoon minced garlic

1 teaspoon dried oregano

2 cups vegetable broth

10-12 fresh basil leaves, chopped

1 teaspoon salt

1 teaspoon pepper

1 teaspoon sugar

½ cup evaporated milk

In a food processor, puree the tomatoes. In a large Dutch oven over medium heat add in 3 tablespoons of oil with the onions and garlic. Cook while stirring for 10 minutes to allow onions to caramelize. Add in the tomatoes, oregano, vegetable broth, basil, salt, pepper and sugar. Stir to combine and bring to a boil for 2 minutes. Cover and reduce heat to low. Simmer for 30 minutes. Add in evaporated milk and simmer for an additional 30 minutes. Serve in the Grilled Cheese Bread Bowl.

Oh' Honey, You're HOT! ...Chicken Sandwich

(Cover Recipe)

2 chicken breasts, cut in half

12-15 spinach leaves

Multigrain bread (or rye or pretzel bread)

Sourdough bread

Marinade:

¼ cup olive oil

¼ cup soy sauce

Juice of 1 lemon

1 tablespoon Dijon mustard

1 tablespoon chili powder

1 teaspoon salt

1 teaspoon pepper

1 teaspoon cayenne pepper

Sauce:

½ cup mayo

3 tablespoons honey

3 tablespoons Dijon mustard

1 tablespoon hot sauce

½ teaspoon salt

In a small bowl, whisk together the marinade ingredients. In a large resealable bag, add the chicken and marinade. Refrigerate for 1½ hours then remove from refrigerator and allow chicken to get to room temperature. This allows the chicken to cook more evenly. While the chicken is marinating, prepare the sauce in a small bowl by whisking together all ingredients. Cover and refrigerate until it is time to build the sandwich. In a large iron skillet over medium high heat, add 2 marinated chicken breasts. Cook on both sides for 8-10 minutes. Remove onto a plate and continue with the remaining two chicken breasts.

To assemble the sandwich: Toast 2 thick slices of your bread of choice, then generously spread the sauce over each slice. Layer one chicken breast and 3-4 fresh spinach leaves on one piece of toast then top with the remaining slice of toast.

Nashville Hot Chicken

2 cups Crisco

2 cups flour

1 tablespoon salt

2 eggs

1 cup milk

2 tablespoons hot sauce

1 whole chicken cut into
10 pieces (breasts cut in half)

2 cups vegetable oil

2 tablespoons cayenne pepper

2 tablespoons brown sugar

1 teaspoon black pepper

½ teaspoon salt

½ teaspoon garlic powder

½ teaspoon paprika

Heat oil in a deep fryer or Dutch oven to 350 degrees. In a large bowl, mix together the flour and 1 tablespoon salt. In a separate large bowl, whisk together the eggs, milk and hot sauce. Take each piece of chicken and do a "double dredge." A double dredge is first coat in egg mixture, then in flour mixture and do over again. Place 3-4 pieces in the oil and fry for 3-4 minutes on each side. Place each piece on a wire rack that is on top of a rimmed cookie sheet. When all of the chicken is fried, place in a 325 degree oven for 10-12 minutes or until internal temperature is 165 degrees. Remove from oven and baste with sauce.

To make sauce: In a small bowl, whisk together the cayenne pepper, brown sugar, black pepper, salt, garlic powder and paprika. Add ½ cup of hot oil from fryer and whisk until well combined. Using a basting brush, cover each piece of chicken with sauce. Serve immediately.

Key Lime Cream Pie

1 prepared graham cracker crust

1 (14 ounce) can sweetened condensed milk

1 (8 ounce) block cream cheese

1 (8 ounce) container whipped cream

½ cup key lime juice (may substitute lime juice)

In a large bowl using a hand mixer, blend together the sweetened condensed milk and the cream cheese until smooth. Add in the whipped cream and continue to blend until it starts to thicken. Add in lime juice and blend until thickened, about 3-5 minutes. Pour into the graham cracker crust and place in the freezer for at least 4 hours to overnight.

KA Note: At this point, it's like Suzanne and I have a mind meld. Because my grandmother—better known as the laziest cook in history (and she'd happily cop to that title)—made a version of this pie (you can find that recipe on my website under "Fake Key Lime Pie"). Of course, Suzanne, being the least lazy cook I know, makes it way better. I mean, cream cheese makes everything better, right? But then adding condensed milk? What? Stop! Lush!

Brownie Lasagna

2 boxes brownie mix

½ cup water

1 ⅓ cups oil

4 eggs

1 (8 ounce) block cream cheese

4 cups powdered sugar

1 teaspoon vanilla extract

¼ cup milk

2 cups milk chocolate chips

1 cup heavy cream

1 chocolate candy bar

Preheat oven to 350 degrees. In a large bowl, mix together the brownie mix, water, oil and eggs until a smooth batter forms. Pour in a parchment lined 9x13-inch baking dish. Bake for 40-45 minutes or until a toothpick comes out clean. Allow to cool completely.

To make the cream cheese frosting layer: In a large bowl using a hand mixer, blend the cream cheese until smooth then add in 1 cup of powdered sugar at a time until blended. Add in the vanilla extract and milk and blend until smooth.

To make the ganache: In a large bowl, place chocolate chips and heavy cream. Stir to combine, then place in the microwave for 2 minutes. Remove from the microwave and stir until all of the chips are melted. If you need additional time in the microwave, go by 30 second increments.

Building the lasagna: Cut the brownie in half widthwise then cut each piece in half horizontally making 4 layers. Place one piece of brownie on a platter and spread a thin layer of ganache on top. Spread about 1/3 of the cream cheese frosting over the ganache then top with another layer of brownie. Repeat layers, topping the final layer with only ganache. Refrigerate for 1 hour before serving. Top with chocolate shavings using a potato peeler and the chocolate candy bar.

Chocolate Chess Pie

1½ cups sugar

3 tablespoons unsweetened cocoa powder

2 eggs

1 (5 ounce) can evaporated milk

¼ cup melted butter

1 teaspoon vanilla extract

1 9-inch unbaked pie crust

Preheat oven to 350 degrees. In a large bowl, mix together the sugar and cocoa. Using a hand mixer, in a small bowl, beat eggs and then add to cocoa mixture. Blend in milk, butter, and vanilla extract. Pour into the pie shell and bake for 1 hour or until set. After 30 minutes, cover the crust edges with foil to prevent burning. Allow to cool before slicing.

When I arrive at it, I find Hawk's Camaro is open, so I slide into the passenger seat.

Apparently, he has some words to share with Brett, and no small amount of them, because it takes about ten minutes before Hawk slides in beside me, starts up the car, and we growl down Brett's lane.

When we're out on the open road, I say, "Thanks for the rescue that I didn't really need."

"Why do you women keep thinking this guy is a good guy?" he murmurs to himself, making zero effort to hide his exasperation. "This guy is not a good guy."

"People are nuanced, Hawk."

"I'm not."

Oh, brother.

He was so nuanced, he almost nuanced himself out of a relationship with his woman due to a big, freaking nuance he was in denial about having.

"No retort?" he prods.

"You aren't *now*. You've found the love of a good woman. So now, you're stable financially. You do work that challenges you with people you like and trust. You've got friends you respect who are loyal to you. And you've got a beautiful family, a wife that adores you to distraction, and you get it regular, and when you do, you get it good. You're welcome for that, by the way."

"Thank you for that, by the way."

"Huh," I huff and cross my arms on my chest.

He leaves it for a beat.

And his voice is *very* different when he adds, "All of it. Thank you for *all* of it, babe."

Oh shit.

He's gonna make me cry.

So of course, I order, "Shut up."

"You brought it up."

"Okay, well, we're shutting up about it now."

"Now who's being a boss?" he mutters.

"I'm not *being* a boss, Hawk. I'm always *the* boss," I declare.

"Right," he says.

Ugh.

Even I can't make myself believe that for more than a second, sitting next to this fucking guy.

Sidestepping that topic, I ask, "Are we going to your house?"

"Yeah, Gwen wants to say hi and the kids wanna see you."

"Does Gwen have homemade cookie dough in the fridge?"

"Is she Gwen?"

"Yes."

"Then what do you think?"

"I think going to your house is acceptable."

"Kit?"

"What?"

"Thank fuck you're such a huge, goddamn pain in the ass and you never gave up."

At that, I turn and slap his biceps.

It's like slapping a pole made of iron.

I mean, my fingers actually hurt.

Wowza.

I get past that and repeat, "I said shut up. You're gonna make me cry. Axl already made me lose half my mascara today. I'm encountering hot guys everywhere. I can't afford to lose any more."

"Just suck it up."

"I can't suck it up. I'm not *nuanced* that way. You have to quit being badass sweet."

"I can't quit being that, you above all people know I'm *nuanced* that way."

Ugh!

"Smartass," I mumble.

"Am I actually having this conversation with you?" he asks.

"Yes."

"Fuck me," he says low.

Ah, if pages could come alive.

No, no, no.

He's Gwen's.

I look out the side window.

After a while, Hawk calls, "Babe."

"Yeah?"

"Was it good being home?"

I turn my head to glance at him before looking forward to face a road that cuts through the immense and indescribable beauty of the mountains of Colorado.

"Always, honey, you know that," I say softly.

Then I sigh and settle into the bucket seat.

Hawk reaches out, takes my hand, and squeezes it before he lets me go.

The pine and aspen slide by.

And I repeat.

"Always."

The End

As we're nearing his house, I have a question to ask Hawk.

So I ask it.

"Do you have any recipes for me?"

Instantly, he busts out laughing.

I grin to myself thinking not only how much I love that sound...

But also, it was worth a try.

Now It's The End

AFTERWORD

KA

I feel, at the end of my first-ever cookbook, it's necessary to mention something very important. Something that, if you read my books, you already know about me.

I love food and I do because food, to me, is about family and friends.

The birth and realization of this cookbook is no different.

You see, Suzanne's "test kitchen," the one I was fortunate enough to participate in, was my friend Liz's kitchen in Florida. And Liz, not incidentally, is Suzanne's sister.

Suzanne would come down from Georgia, lugging massive amounts of food in tow, and she'd cook for us...for hours.

Hours.

Sometimes, Liz and I would leave her alone to do her thing.

Sometimes, Liz and I would sit and chat with her.

Most of the time, we all had wine.

One of these times, Liz's husband, Steve, who I utterly adore, but who has the palate of a three-year-old (one day, I may share the story of Steve accidentally biting into a slice of my fig, goat cheese and prosciutto pizza, the results not being pretty...for Steve, but they were hilarious...for Liz and me), kept us regaled with his usual hilarity.

In this instance, going on and on and on about his favorite dessert... "Puddin' Pie."

Now, Chicklets, Suzanne is making gourmet deviled eggs and bruschetta and bacon knots, and when I say this, she's been cooking for eight freaking hours, and Steve wants her to make "Puddin' Pie," which is a store-bought pie crust filled with boxed chocolate pudding.

The woman is sprinkling cotija cheese on top of deviled eggs with an eagle eye akin to Van Gogh painting a sunflower and Steve wants her to whip up boxed pudding.

Needless to say, watching these two interact, I'm almost paralytic with laughter.

In the end, she shares the kitchen while Steve makes his pie.

Because she loves him.

That's what it's all about.

And straight up, that Puddin' Pie did not suck.

These, my Chicklets, are precious memories.

And from those, the words and the food in this book, from Suzanne and me to you, is a labor of love.

I hope you open this book often and make these recipes for your family and friends and create your own precious memories.

I hope that with all my heart.

PS: I mention food in my books often. And if I have the recipe, I post it on my website. So if you want more, feel free to peruse my beloved family and life recipes here: https://www.kristenashley.net/encore/recipes/

PPS: For more awesomeness from Suzanne, and her cadre of author friends (who also are mine), be certain to find her Southern Bits and Bites series, as well as the books she's done with Lexi Blake, Larissa Ione, J. Kenner, and Kristen Proby. For ease to get you this goodness, a list of these are at the end of this book.

Dream Team Series

Evie and Mag – *Dream Maker* (available)

Boone and Ryn – *Dream Chaser* (at publication of this cookbook, as yet unpublished, releasing December 22, 2020)

Hattie and Axl – *Dream Spinner* (at publication of this cookbook, as yet unpublished, releasing Summer 2021)

Pepper and Auggie – (Title TBD: at publication of this cookbook, as yet unpublished, releasing Winter 2021)

Brett "Cisco" Rappaport, all of the above.

Chaos Series

Hound – *Wild Like the Wind* (available)

High and Millie – *Walk through Fire* (available)

Dream Man Series

Hawk and Gwen Delgado, Elvira – *Mystery Man* (available)

Tack and Tyra Allen (and Elvira) – *Motorcycle Man* and Chaos Series (all available)

Lottie and Mo Morrison – *Quiet Man* (available)

Rock Chick

Tex, Duke, Indy, Lee, Ally, Jet, Eddie, Sadie Daisy, Shirleen, Smithie, Ray, Tod and Stevie, Slick.

All ten titles in the Rock Chick series are available.

ROCK CHICK SERIES:

Rock Chick

Rock Chick Rescue

Rock Chick Redemption

Rock Chick Renegade

Rock Chick Revenge

Rock Chick Reckoning

Rock Chick Regret

Rock Chick Revolution

Rock Chick Reawakening

Rock Chick Reborn

THE 'BURG SERIES:

For You

At Peace

Golden Trail

Games of the Heart

The Promise

Hold On

THE CHAOS SERIES:

Own the Wind

Fire Inside

Ride Steady

Walk Through Fire

A Christmas to Remember

Rough Ride

Wild Like the Wind

Free

THE COLORADO MOUNTAIN SERIES:

The Gamble
Sweet Dreams
Lady Luck
Breathe
Jagged
Kaleidoscope
Bounty

DREAM MAN SERIES:

Mystery Man
Wild Man
Law Man
Motorcycle Man
Quiet Man

DREAM TEAM SERIES:

Dream Maker
Dream Chaser

THE FANTASYLAND SERIES:

Wildest Dreams
The Golden Dynasty
Fantastical
Broken Dove
Midnight Soul

THE HONEY SERIES:

The Deep End
The Farthest Edge
The Greatest Risk

THE MAGDALENE SERIES:

The Will
Soaring
The Time in Between

MOONLIGHT AND MOTOR OIL SERIES:

The Hookup
The Slow Burn

THE THREE SERIES:

Until the Sun Falls from the Sky
With Everything I Am
Wild and Free

THE UNFINISHED HERO SERIES:

Knight
Creed
Raid
Deacon
Sebring

GHOSTS AND REINCARNATION SERIES:

Sommersgate House
Lacybourne Manor
Penmort Castle
Fairytale Come Alive
Lucky Stars

THE RISING SERIES:

The Beginning of Everything
The Plan Commences
The Dawn of the End
The Rising

MATHILDA, SUPERWITCH:

Mathilda's Book of Shadows
Mathilda The Rise of the Dark Lord

OTHER TITLES BY KRISTEN ASHLEY:

Heaven and Hell
Play It Safe
Three Wishes
Complicated
Loose Ends
Fast Lane

All titles by Kristen Ashley can be purchased on her website: kristenashley.net.

OTHER BOOKS BY SUZANNE M. JOHNSON

Southern Bits & Bites
Southern Kid Bits & Mom Bites
Southern Bits & Bites: Our 150 Favorite Recipes

WRITING WITH LEXI BLAKE

Master Bits & Mercenary Bites
Master Bits & Mercenary Bites~Girls Night

WRITING WITH J. KENNER

Bar Bites: A Man of the Month Cookbook

WRITING WITH KRISTEN PROBY

Indulge With Me: A With Me in Seattle Celebration

WRITING WITH LARISSA IONE

Dining with Angels: Bits & Bites from the Demonica Universe

INDEX

SALADS

SAUCES & SEASONINGS

ABOUT THE AUTHOR: KRISTEN ASHLEY

Kristen Ashley is the *New York Times* bestselling author of over seventy romance novels including the Rock Chick, Colorado Mountain, Dream Man, Chaos, Unfinished Heroes, The 'Burg, Magdalene, Fantasyland, The Three, Ghost and Reincarnation, The Rising, Dream Team and Honey series along with several standalone novels. She's a hybrid author, publishing titles both independently and traditionally, her books have been translated in fourteen languages and she's sold over three million books.

Kristen's novel, *Law Man,* won the RT Book Reviews Reviewer's Choice Award for best Romantic Suspense, her independently published title *Hold On* was nominated for RT Book Reviews best Independent Contemporary Romance, and her traditionally published title *Breathe* was nominated for best Contemporary Romance. Kristen's titles *Motorcycle Man, The Will,* and *Ride Steady* (which won the Reader's Choice award from Romance Reviews) all made the final rounds for Goodreads Choice Awards in the Romance category.

Kristen, born in Gary and raised in Brownsburg, Indiana, was a fourth generation graduate of Purdue University. Since, she has lived in Denver, the West Country of England, and she now resides in Phoenix. She worked as a charity executive for eighteen years prior to beginning her independent publishing career. She now writes full-time.

Although romance is her genre, the prevailing themes running through all of Kristen's novels are friendship, family, and a strong sisterhood. To this end, and as a way to thank her readers for their support, Kristen has created the Rock Chick Nation, a series of programs that are designed to give back to her readers and promote a strong female community.

The mission of the Rock Chick Nation is to live your best life, be true to your true self, recognize your beauty, and last but definitely not least, take your sister's back whether they're at your side as friends and family or if they're thousands of miles away and you don't know who they are.

The programs of the RC Nation include Rock Chick Rendezvous, weekends Kristen organizes full of parties and get-togethers to bring the sisterhood together, Rock Chick Recharges, evenings Kristen arranges for women who have been nominated to receive a special night, and Rock Chick Rewards, an ongoing program that raises funds for nonprofit women's organizations Kristen's readers nominate. Kristen's Rock Chick Rewards have donated over $146,000 to charity and this number continues to rise.

You can read more about Kristen, her titles and the Rock Chick Nation at KristenAshley.net.

CONNECT WITH KRISTEN ASHLEY

Official Website: www.kristenashley.net

Kristen's Facebook Page: www.facebook.com/kristenashleybooks

Follow Kristen on Twitter: @KristenAshley68

Discover Kristen's Pins on Pinterest: www.pinterest.com/kashley0155

Follow Kristen on Instagram: KristenAshleyBooks

ABOUT THE AUTHOR: SUZANNE JOHNSON

Suzanne Johnson is the *USA Today* bestselling author of three cookbooks, and the recipe developer for six other books with: Lexi Blake, J. Kenner, Kristen Proby, Larissa Ione, and Kristen Ashley. A family-trained south Georgia chef, Suzanne has been cooking all her life, creating not only unique food, but precious memories of meals shared with family and friends. In all her books, Suzanne shows that making delicious meals doesn't have to be complicated—they just have to be made with love.

CONNECT WITH SUZANNE JOHNSON

Website: http://southernbitsandbites.com/

Facebook: https://www.facebook.com/Southern-Bits-Bites-352580344928317

Instagram: southernbitsand_bites